Hangtown

Of what use is a deserted ghost town? None at all unless like the old desert rat, Josh Banks and his young partner, Wage Carson, you have nowhere else to go and are tired of sleeping out with the rattlesnakes. In Hangtown, at least, they would have some shelter from the elements, some water for their weary mounts. In the spirit of things the two saddle bums vote Josh mayor of Hangtown and appoint Wage town marshal.

They weren't alone for long. Within days the painted ladies arrived, followed by a detachment of soldiers. Things were already out of control when four rough-looking strangers arrived seeking a brief respite from the harsh desert. There was to be no respite for any of them, especially for Josh and Marshal Carson. It was not long before gunplay erupted and the silent town was prodded to violent life.

By the same author

Overland Stage
Dakota Skies
Incident at Coyote Wells
Dark Angel Riding
Rogue Law
The Land Grabbers
On The Great Plains

Hangtown

LOGAN WINTERS

A Black Horse Western

ROBERT HALE · LONDON

© Logan Winters 2009
First published in Great Britain 2009

ISBN 978-0-7090-8795-3

Robert Hale Limited
Clerkenwell House
Clerkenwell Green
London EC1R 0HT

www.halebooks.com

Typeset by
Derek Doyle & Associates, Shaw Heath
Printed and bound in Great Britain by
CPI Antony Rowe, Chippenham and Eastbourne

ONE

'Well, isn't this something?' Josh Banks said dismally. He sat his white-eared mule in the middle of the street of the dead desert town. Above the two men the red mesa jutted skyward, casting its deep shadow over them.

'The man who drew the map seemed to know what he was talking about,' Wage Carson answered unhappily. They looked around them at the boarded-up windows, broken awning supports and collapsed plank walks.

'Well, I guess he did, because here we are,' Josh said sadly. He swung down from his mule and stood massaging his cramped leg.

'Wonder where everyone went,' Wage Carson said, looking across the deserted ghost town as the rising wind lifted yellow dust. His gray horse shifted its feet uneasily. They had been riding long and hard and had expected to find food and water, human company here.

'The wind probably blew 'em away,' Josh said as the gusts continued to increase. He shrugged, 'Who knows why these towns grow up or why they die. I think there was a little silver ore up there.' He lifted his whiskered chin toward the bulk of the mesa, 'And it just petered out.'

'Do you think that it was the fever that did it?' Wage Carson asked with trepidation.

'Who knows?' the older man said. 'For now, let's see if we can find some water. There must have been a water source here . . . once.'

Or, he was thinking, perhaps that was the reason the town had died. Maybe the water had just dried up, and nothing lived out on the desert without a source of water.

'Where?' young Wage Carson asked the bearded man. 'Where do we look, Josh?' The big-shouldered bear of a man was not more than twenty years old. He could bend iron with his bare hands, but he looked to the scrawny Josh Banks for advice always.

'First, any local business. If we can't find a working pump, then we look around the base of the mesa. That's where water is most likely to be

6

seeping. We don't need enough to support a town, just enough for us and our mounts.'

'We were right,' Wage said as they walked the dusty street, 'this is the place.'

He had kicked over a fallen plank sign on which was ineptly painted 'Hangtown Commerce Bank'.

'Well,' Josh Banks said tugging at his silver beard, 'we were right about where we were. The question now is, what in hell are we going to do about it?'

Wage Carson turned and surveyed the empty street with its skeletons of buildings, shuttered establishments and treeless lanes and scratched his head as if probing for an idea. 'I know what we can do,' Wage Carson said finally, a boyish grin on his face.

'Any idea, I'm willing to hear it,' Josh Banks said. He had removed his hat to wipe the perspiration from his forehead. The dry wind lifted his shaggy gray hair.

'Joshua, my old trail friend – don't you see!' Wage Carson turned in a tight circle, his big hands raised skyward. 'We now own us a town.'

Josh Banks frowned thoughtfully. He supposed that Wage was right in a way, but even if they did, what in the world was to be done with it?

Hangtown was dead. Hangtown, population 2, was not a livelier proposition.

'Let's find some water,' Josh growled, but in his mind the wheels were turning.

Owning their own town was surely something. Better than owning only the mule he sat on.

It gave a man pause to consider.

They were able to find a little seep east of the town where the great mesa's shadows lay heavy and cool, and there they allowed their mounts to drink their fill. Sprawled on his back, hands behind his head, Wage Carson commented:

'It's a shame that the work of man falls into disuse.'

'Meaning?' Josh Banks was seated on a large, flat-topped rock, watching his mule drink.

'Like I already said, Josh – here is this entire town men labored to build, with a lot of sweat and maybe a little blood. Now it sits empty and forgotten. I'm still thinking we ought to claim it. It must be good for something!'

'Such as?' Josh asked.

'I don't know,' Wage said to the older man with a shake of his head. 'But it is shame to let. . . .'

Josh Banks was tired; he let the kid's words flow past unheeded. Wage did have a point of sorts. They could rest up here with plenty of water for their mounts, with a roof over their heads. They were in no hurry to get anywhere and they had been long on the trail.

'. . . Find out what the law really is in a situation like this,' Wage was saying.

'It's something to consider,' Josh Banks said, rising from the stone to dust off the seat of his jeans. 'For now, let's get out of the sun and see what we can scrape up to eat.'

There was a hotel in the ghost town. Not much of a place, but it seemed sound. With dusk settling they threw their saddles down in the cobwebbed lobby and looked around. Two front windows were broken out and the dry desert wind whistled through. Upstairs were six small rooms with musty bedding. The cots were relatively comfortable, and it would sure beat spending yet another night on the open ground with snakes and scorpions for company. There were lanterns, but the kerosene seemed to have leaked out or evaporated. An emergency supply of candles was discovered in an upstairs utility closet. They lit four of these to burn in the room they had chosen and their flickering light offered some small solace against the settling night. Outside the wind had begun to build, and it rattled the windows as the cold desert night darkened the land. But in their bedrolls spread over tick mattresses they were as safe and comfortable as they had been for days.

Josh Banks fell to sleep thinking that maybe the kid was not so dumb after all. There were worse fates than owning your own town.

Morning dawned cool and bright. Only a few wisps of pinkish clouds colored the high skies. The old mule Josh Banks rode and Wage Carson's gray horse were picketed out in the long grass behind the town where they had discovered the flowing water. The two men were left to consider their position again.

They had shifted two old but serviceable chairs from the dusty hotel lobby out on to the plankwalk where they sat, indolently enjoying the warmth of the rising sun. Josh had his stubby pipe lighted, and he squinted up and down the street through narrowed eyes. Wage had his hat tugged low against the glare of the morning light.

'Well, here we are,' Josh said at length. 'And what have we got?'

'Roof over our heads,' Wage said, stretching his thick arms lazily.

'Yes, but Wage, that is about it. It won't sustain us long.'

'We don't even know that,' Wage said, leaning

forward, rough hands clenched together. 'There could be all sorts of useful items strewn about – things people were in too much of a hurry to cart off. There might even be some silver ore left in that lode – little enough to profit them so that they gave up on mining it, but enough to see us through a winter. If we could find some tools, we could take a look.'

Josh Banks just nodded. His younger companion had more ambition, higher hopes than he did. 'We don't even know what happened here, Wage. I've an idea—' he jabbed the stem of his pipe in the direction of the squat yellow building across the street. A barely legible tilted sign hung on its face could be seen there. '*Hangtown Sentinel*,' it read.

'What's that?' Wage asked.

'Newspaper office. I guess in its heyday there was enough population in Hangtown to support one.'

'What did you want to do?' Wage asked with a laugh. 'Get the morning edition?'

'No,' Josh said with one of his infrequent smiles, 'but there might be some back issues left around, why would anyone want to take them away? Maybe we can get an idea of what happened here, why everybody just pulled up stakes and left.'

'It's a thought,' Wage said, 'then maybe we can poke around and see if anyone left any food behind. If not, I'll be grazing in the grass with our mounts before the day is out.' He rubbed his belly.

'We'll find us a deer,' Josh said confidently. 'Didn't you notice those tracks up along the seep yesterday?'

'I guess I didn't,' Wage replied. He hadn't seen the deer sign or noticed the newspaper office. He had to give it to Josh Banks. The old man was keener of sight, and maybe more clever than he himself was. That was why they made a good team of saddle partners, Wage decided. Josh did the thinking and Wage did most of the work. It made it easier on both of them.

They crossed the street under clear skies, a light wind bending the branches of the solitary cottonwood tree in the town square – someone's idea of adding permanence to a town which could never have had the chance at anything but a passing existence.

Clumping up on to the sagging boardwalk opposite, the two went to the front door of the *Hangtown Sentinel* office. There was a lock on the door, but Wage was easily able to shoulder his way inside. Josh followed. There was nothing in the office; no printing press, no desks, no chairs. But strewn around the room were yellowed copies of the town's one-sheet newspaper. Josh bent and picked one up. Carrying it to the greasy window he scanned it. Wage who had never learned to read, waited.

'What's it say?' he asked finally.

'Pretty much what we thought, though the man had a flowery way with words.' Josh Banks leaned against the wall and read: *This being the final issue of the paper founded with such high expectations. . . .* 'No sense wading through all of this,' Josh said. 'Just a sentence or two pretty much tells the story.'

With the exhaustion of the silver seam which many had hoped would provide for the area's prosperity. . . .

Again Josh paused. 'Here is the matter in a nutshell, Wage:'

With the first of the prospectors having struck their tents and the last of the hopeful settlers surrendering Hangtown to its inevitable demise, wagons heaped with their poor belongings, the column of dejected pilgrims. . . .

'It goes on a while more but don't say anything much,' Josh said, letting the newspaper flutter to the floor. 'Silver ran out; town's deserted. Which we had kind of figured already.'

Wage watched the old man stifle a yawn. 'What do you think?' Wage asked, as they went out again into the brilliant morning sunshine.

'About what?' Josh asked. The utter silence of the town was beginning to spook him a little. The loudest sound to be heard was the dry wind rattling the leaves of the cottonwood tree.

'You know,' Wage Carson said with eagerness. 'The town – can we keep it for our own?'

'Is it worth the having?' Josh Banks asked, looking around.

'I don't know,' the younger man said. 'But, Josh, we had nothing where we came from and we are going nowhere. We've at least got a roof, water, and like you said I can knock down a deer now and then for food. It seems to me it beats riding the long trail again with winter coming on.'

'You do have a point,' Josh said, placing a gnarled hand on his companion's shoulder. 'The open trail's getting harder on me as the years pass.' He shrugged, 'Why not at least give it a try? Let's look around a little more.'

They next tried the old jail house. There was nothing much there. Cell doors standing open, an empty gunrack. There was, however, a dilapidated desk with one broken leg. Three or four ancient wanted posters were tacked to the wall. Wage Carson rummaged through the desk. He stood with a shiny object in his hand.

'Look, Josh – a town marshal's badge. Can I keep it?'

'Might as well pin it on,' Josh said with a shrug. His young, bull-shouldered partner sometimes had a childish side to him. Just a big, half-smart, good-natured kid. Josh Banks had been half-kidding, but Wage pinned the badge on his faded blue shirt with delight.

'Is this official?' Wage asked.

'Unless we can find someone who objects,' Josh answered.

'I know!' Wage said, animated now. 'We can make you mayor and you can appoint me to office.'

'I accept the office of mayor,' Josh Banks said tolerantly. 'What about holding an election first, though?'

'Oh, Josh,' Wage said, nearly blushing. 'We can hold that here and now. I'll vote for you.'

Josh smiled. What the hell, he might as well become mayor of a ghost town. It was the highest office he was ever likely to hold. If it made Wage happy to be officially appointed, the hell with it – why not?

It was time, however, to get on with more practical matters. They had shelter, water, it shouldn't take much to hunt a deer. The animals probably hadn't seen a human being in years and would not be wary of hunters. Then, Josh considered, it would be a good idea to take their mounts to the shelter of the stable, after they had checked it out and seen what kind of shape it was in. Josh smiled, lit up his stubby pipe and slapped Wage Carson on the shoulder.

'Marshal, let's see what needs to be done around town. It's my duty as mayor, after all. You just make sure that you keep the peace in Hangtown.'

That was said lightly, but it would prove to be much more difficult than either man could have imagined.

TWO

By early afternoon Josh and Wage Carson had the old stable respectably clean and they led the mule and Wage's gray horse into the shaded building. Earlier Wage, prowling around in the hotel, had discovered a working kitchen pump and a collection of tinned goods. Few of the cans had any labels, and most of the tins were dented, probably the reason they had been left behind. It didn't matter what was in them; they now had food, shelter, water and graze for their horses. Again Josh Banks reflected that maybe owning an empty town wasn't so bad. It was at least preferable to spending the nights on the long desert trail without hope of finding adequate water or provisions. Which was the way they had been living.

Early in the afternoon with the white sun holding high, the wagons rolled into Hangtown.

There were two of them and Josh and Wage, roused by the sounds of creaking axle hubs went out into the street to take a look. Peering into the brilliance of the desert day they saw a four-passenger surrey pulled by two black horses and, on its heels, stirring up fountains of white dust, an ancient Conestoga covered wagon.

The two men started that way. The wagons pulled up in front of the hotel. The horses, dusty and beat down, were panting for water, stamping impatient feet, showing angry eyes at the tribulations of their journey.

'My Lord, Josh,' Wage Carson said, 'it's women!'

'That's what they are,' the old man replied. As they approached the hotel they saw two of the new arrivals standing on the boardwalk, looking around in disbelief. One of these was the matronly sort in a dark dress, wearing a tiny black hat. Beside her was a slender young slip of a girl in jeans and a white shirt. The sound of the men's approaching boots on the boardwalk caused their heads to turn toward Josh and Wage. Wage

18

Carson had not failed to notice the two other women, middle-aged and weary-looking sitting on the surrey seats. A raw-looking man of advancing years sat on the Conestoga's unsprung seat. He was hunched forward, staring vacantly at the ground. His eyes were as weary as those of the horses he had been driving.

'Hey, you,' the broad-faced woman called as Josh and Carson approached, 'is this place open for business or not?'

'All depends on how you look at it,' Josh replied. 'Let me introduce myself, I am Mayor Josh Bank, and this is Marshal Wage Carson.' Wage beamed at the form of introduction, though he kept his eyes shyly turned away. The big woman was intimidating, and the little sawed-off one in blue jeans looked petrified at the sight of the hulking 'marshal'.

'How should I look at it?' the big woman asked with a deep-throated chuckle. The dry wind rustled her heavy dark skirts.

'It's like this,' Josh said, removing his hat to mop his brow with his red bandanna. 'The place hasn't seen much business lately. The town had to take it over. There's shelter for you and . . . your ladies, but you might not find it up to your expectations.'

19

'What about the soldiers?' the big woman asked. 'Where is everyone?'

'I don't know anything about any soldiers,' Josh said honestly.

'Look,' the matron went on – the other women had clambered down from the surrey and were stretching – 'my name is Cora Kellogg. A few years back we always stayed in Hangtown for a little while – around the time of the month the soldiers from Fort Thomas got paid. You know,' Wage could have sworn that she winked at Josh, 'lonely boys out here, they always like to have someone to talk to.'

'I'm afraid times have changed,' Josh answered a little stiffly.

'Yes, well . . . we took our show on the road,' Cora Kellogg answered, looking up and down the empty streets. Wage found the courage to ask:

'You are entertainers, then?'

'In a manner of speaking,' the matron answered. She waved at the hotel again. 'You say we can rest up here for awhile, though?'

'Do as you like,' Josh answered. 'The marshal and I have one room – the rest are available, but I'm afraid you might have to do some cleaning up before you can use them.'

'Cora!' The voice came from a red-headed

woman of thirty or so. Her face was as pale as the desert sand. 'We have to find a place! I have got to get out of the sun or die.'

'I'll take care of it, Rebecca,' Cora Kellogg said impatiently. 'All right, mister mayor, we'll see to ourselves. The ladies have been long on the trail. Liza!' The dark-haired sawn-off girl lifted nervous eyes. 'Get into the wagon and see what kind of cleaning gear we have. Then' – Cora had opened the door to the cob-webbed, musty hotel lobby – 'see what you can do to make the place habitable.'

'Mister mayor,' Cora asked, and now there was a hint of mockery in her voice, 'is there a place we can stable and water our horses? It's been a long trail. My man, Gus, there, will see to the harnesses.'

'I think we can accommodate the horses,' Josh said. Wage thought he detected concern now in Josh's eyes. The three ladies trekked into the hotel, uttering disappointed sounds. The other girl, the little one – Liza – was rummaging around in the back of the big covered wagon, searching for some sort of supplies. The man, Gus, just sat on his bench seat stolidly as if time had already done all it could to him.

'Why don't you help the man out, Wage? After he has dropped the harnesses, you can show him

21

where the seep water is. Don't forget to take your rifle,' Josh advised, 'we still need to get us a deer. You might just see one up there, though it's the wrong time of day'

'All right,' Wage agreed, his broad face now unhappy. 'These women – I wonder. . . .'

'Don't worry about them, Wage,' Josh told him. 'They won't be around long. What's to keep them here?'

The women had found lantern oil somewhere, for as dusk settled, the hotel began to glow with light. Josh crossed that way, curiously, and entering he found the lobby dusted, swept and waxed. That little girl, Liza, was busy still, cleaning up behind the desk. She rose with cobwebs in her hair and watched Josh Banks's approach with wide, dark, emotionless eyes.

'You women have done a good job in here,' Josh said by way of compliment. The girl's expression did not change, nor did she answer. Shrugging, Josh climbed the stairs to his room. Passing an open door he glanced in to see the other three women reclining in chairs, fixing their hair, dressed still in their finery.

He mentally apologized to Liza: it was pretty obvious who had done all of the cleaning up.

Behind the hotel Wage Carson had hung a deer carcass from an oak tree and was busy skinning it out. He glanced to the darkening skies, hoping that he would have enough light to finish his chore.

His big shoulders ached, his hands were bloody. Taking down the four-point buck had been no problem, but without a horse he had been obliged to carry it back to town. Leaving it out there while he returned for his pony would have been an open invitation to the coyotes and other scavengers. Wage was not complaining. He had performed more difficult tasks in his time, and at least now they had meat. All of the tins they had so far opened had contained only beans, and that diet could get mighty thin after a while.

A patch of light flashed across the yard as the back door to the hotel opened. The small woman with the short dark hair appeared there and began vigorously shaking a dust mop. Wage stood watching her, his skinning knife still in his hand. The girl stopped and stood with her shoulder leaning against one of the uprights that supported the rear porch. She looked small, forlorn and very tired.

Wage considered offering her one of the deer's

haunches so that the women might have roast venison to eat – they must be hungry, too. He knew that he was only making an excuse: he wanted to talk to the girl. Shy as he was, Wage started that way, before she could go back into the hotel.

'Anything wrong, miss?' Wage asked, and the girl started as he emerged from the shadows. A stray lanternlight beam caught the silver badge on his shirt and the girl relaxed.

'Oh, it's you, Marshal,' Liza said, thrusting fingers into her hair. 'You startled me.'

'I'm sorry, I didn't mean to,' Wage said. Then his usual tongue-tied manner around women returned and he was unable to think of anything else to say.

'What were you doing out there?' Liza asked, a little trepidation returning as she recognized the stains on Wage's hands for what they were.

'That's why I came over,' Wage said, remembering his excuse. 'I shot a deer up along the seep, and I've been butchering it. I thought you ladies could probably use some fresh meat.' Then he fell silent again, looking away, his posture awkward and shy as a boy at his first dance.

'Venison steaks would be a fine change from

what we've been dining on lately,' Liza said, using her fingers to brush her hair back from her forehead. 'If I can find enough wood to get the kitchen stove going.'

'You do the cooking, too?' Wage asked, studying the girl's dark eyes by the scattered lamplight.

'I have to earn my keep,' Liza replied.

Wage nodded. He didn't quite understand why only Liza was required to earn her keep, but he had run out of words and only said, 'I'll bring you a haunch. Are there any butcher knives in that kitchen?'

'I'll make do,' Liza said. As Wage turned his back and started away he heard the small voice behind him add, 'Thank you, Marshal'

Without turning to face her, Wage said, 'I'll see what I can find in the way of firewood.'

Then the yard grew darker again as the door was shut. Wage looked back toward the hotel, watching the lighted windows where, once, a slender silhouette passed. He realized as he returned to his work and did what he could in haste, that the desert was suddenly full of questions. He would have to talk seriously to Josh Banks.

*

Just as dusk was turning to purple night, with only a few pennants of pale color in the western sky, the stars already blinking on one by one, the lone rider appeared at the head of the dusty street and guided his pony toward the lighted hotel. His mount was a high-stepping bay, but it showed some signs of weariness. The rider wore cavalry blue.

Cora Kellogg and the pale Rebecca had seated themselves in front of the hotel, enjoying the cool of evening when the horseman, leaving a trail of white dust behind him, slowed his horse and approached them. Cora blinked, squinted her eyes to focus and then lifted her heavy body with a smile and a cry of welcome.

'Private Dan Osborne! I don't believe it.'

'Corporal Osborne, Cora,' the narrow young man said, tapping his chevrons. 'It's been a few years, don't forget!' He swung down from his trail-weary horse and approached the porch, tilting back his cap, propping one boot up on the edge of the plankwalk. 'And – I don't believe it, either! Is that Rebecca? My God? And Madeline is still with you? When did you get back? I used to pass through Hangtown hoping to see you girls again, but then the place just finally gave up its ghost to the desert.'

'We just arrived today,' Cora said. 'But you, Osborne, you're still at Fort Thomas after all this time?'

'I am,' Dan Osborne said. 'My years in the service have made me too lazy to consider honest work again.' He grinned as he told Cora that. 'I ride dispatch these days. It lets me get out on my own without any officers looking me over.'

'I'm surprised Fort Thomas is still there,' Cora said. Now the pale, red-haired woman had moved up beside Cora and she tried a wan smile that was meant to be warmer than it was. Rebecca was still exhausted from the long trail.

Cora Kellogg knew that outposts were constructed and then abandoned as the Indian menace grew and then abated and the forts became useless in the push west. There were dozens of these standing empty across the far lands.

'We're still there,' Osborne said cheerfully.

'Are you going to stay the night?' Rebecca asked. She seemed relieved when the answer came:

'I'd love to, Princess, but I have a dispatch for my commanding officer that is marked "urgent". I've got to try to make Fort Thomas tonight.' He paused and grinned again, 'But I will be back –

now that you ladies are here. Don't make any plans. The first of the month, payday, is the day after tomorrow: a lot of the boys you remember from the old days will be wanting to pay you a visit.'

Josh Banks, standing at his open hotel window heard half of this exchange, enough to cause him to frown. He wondered if they had a town ordinance against this sort of activity. Of course they did not: he and Wage were the town. He wondered if they should enact one. Josh was no prude, but he had believed the women were going to get tired of the ghost town and leave shortly. Now with the promise of money, it seemed doubtful that Cora and her girls would be pulling out any time soon. It smelled like trouble to Josh Banks. Men, loose women and money were always a bad combination. He was glad there was no whiskey to be had in Hangtown, because that was usually the fuse that lit the combustible mix.

He turned and made his way downstairs, emerging from the hotel as the dust stirred up by the departing soldier's pony still hung in the air. The two women still sat in their chairs on the porch. The older, darker one, Cora Kellogg glanced up and said, 'Good evening, Mayor

Banks.' Josh wasn't sure if he had detected a note of sarcasm in her voice or not. He only nodded, turned on his heel and started out looking for Wage Carson.

He wasn't hard to find. Behind the hotel, working in the dusky dimness, he was just finishing cleaning and skinning the deer he had shot. A little yellow light bled through the windows at the back of the hotel. Crossing the shadowed yard Josh approached Wage who heard him coming, lowered his knife and turned to greet him.

'How's it going?' Josh inquired.

'All right,' Wage said. 'I could have used another hour of daylight, though.' Josh nodded. It was also starting to grow cool out, the desert temperature plummeting as night crept in. 'Josh,' Wage told him, 'I promised that little girl a haunch of venison.'

'That's all right with me,' Josh answered. 'You're the one doing the work anyway.'

Wage started to return to his butchering, then paused again. He stammered a little as he said, 'Josh. Don't it seem that they're sort of abusing that girl? I mean, it seems to me she's doing every bit of the heavy lifting.'

'I noticed that myself,' Josh answered. 'But it's

their business and none of ours.'

'I know, but still. . . .' Wage glanced toward the lighted kitchen window and Josh Banks saw a glimmering of the oldest human yearning in the young man's eyes. He smiled a little sadly. The big kid knew nothing of the world, nothing of women, and it seemed he was setting himself up for trouble. However, there was no way in the world a man, or woman, could be cautioned once they had their minds set that way.

'What I'm uneasy about,' Josh said, only partially changing the subject, 'is that it now seems that the women have it in mind to settle in here for more than a few days. There was a pony soldier passing through on his way to Fort Thomas. I heard him say he'd be coming back with some of his friends after payday.'

'I don't like the sound of that,' Wage said frowning. 'What are we supposed to do with them when they get here? We can't feed 'em. They'll be wanting to stay in the hotel too, and I don't think it's right to have them bunking that near to the ladies.'

Josh agreed, although the older man believed the soldiers had in mind bunking closer than 'near' to the ladies. 'I guess we're going to have to do some brain work, Wage. Maybe pass a couple of town ordinances about these things. Of course,' he reminded Wage, 'you being the marshal, you're the one who would have to enforce any law we come up with. It might not be easy.'

Wage stood frowning, then he shrugged his big shoulders. 'It's either we do that or we just ride off ourselves, isn't it?'

'That's about the only two choices we have. I thought the women would just stay a night, maybe two to rest up. Now. . . .' Josh sighed again, more heavily. 'Running a town isn't going to be as easy as I'd thought.'

'I guess not.' Wage was silent for a minute, standing in the near-darkness, his skinning knife still in his hand. 'What you're suggesting, Josh, is it legal? For us to pass town ordinances, I mean?'

'We're the only two permanent residents of Hangtown. I guess we can do what we damn well please,' Josh said, although conviction was lacking in his tone. 'If we mean to stay on, we have to do something more than strut around telling ourselves what important men we are.'

'All right.' Wage smiled crookedly. 'I guess we'll have to call a meeting between the two of us and vote on the few laws we might wish to make.'

'That's it,' Josh said, clapping the big man's

shoulder. His expression was still a little grim as he told Wage Carson, 'There's a cot in the marshal's office and leather-strap bunks in both of the jail cells. For me, I'm in favor of moving our gear out of the hotel and sleeping there. You can do what you want.'

'I'll go along with you whatever you say, Josh. You know that,' the big man said sincerely. He hesitated. 'You think that maybe tomorrow we should clean the office up . . . and make sure we have the keys to the cells?'

'I'm afraid that we must do that, Wage. When the soldiers get here, who knows what might happen. Unless,' Josh said again 'you want just to saddle up and shed this Hangtown dust.'

Wage was looking again toward the lighted kitchen window of the hotel. The same look lingered in his hound-dog eyes. 'No, Josh. I think we ought to give it a try at least. I'm for staying on. For at least a little while more.'

Josh nodded. What Wage had in mind was one thing he never gave a man advice about. It had never come up with the youngster before, but here it was, it seemed, circling in his mind and singing in his blood like white doves and summer roses. 'I'll start over toward the marshal's office,' Josh Banks said. 'I'll sweep up a little and see if I can maybe find a lantern.'

'All right, Josh,' Wage said, although he was barely listening to the old man. 'I'll take the girl her venison and then pack up our gear.'

Josh started away, unsure if this was a wise decision. It was either Hangtown or the long dry desert, however, and Josh was trailed-out. He was too old for those long desert rides.

He walked out on to the main street and started toward the marshal's office. The sound of approaching horses brought his head up. What now? He stepped back into the shadows of a buckled awning to watch as the four tough-looking men rode into Hangtown.

THREE

The four new arrivals rode desert-beat horses. All carried guns, all were bearded to one degree or the other. They halted their weary animals near the stable and looked around in puzzlement. Josh Banks started that way.

'Evening, men,' Josh said. At the sound of his voice one of the strangers dropped his hand toward his holstered belt gun. The rider next to him gripped his fellow rider's wrist and shook his head.

'What the hell happened here?' a bulky rider who seemed to be the leader demanded.

'Silver played out, most everybody left – years ago,' Josh explained.

'I'll be damned. Bert, you said—'

'It was a standing town the last time I was up

this way, Jay,' a narrower rider answered.

'There's lights on up there,' the man called Jay said, pointing toward the hotel.

'That's going to be an army billet,' Josh said, stretching the truth. 'We're cleaning it up for the soldiers.' He saw the glances that passed between the men at the mention of the army. They looked far too rough for Josh's liking. He had been thinking that maybe speaking of the army might convince them to move on, or at least to restrain their impulses which might become reckless should they happen to spot a silk skirt.

'Army billet?' the man called Jay asked, scowling down from his exhausted horse's back.

'A dozen or so men from Fort Thomas. There's been some Indian trouble nearby, and they're going to be staying in Hangtown for a while.'

'Is that so? And just who are you?' Jay asked, his eyes narrowing.

Josh laughed. 'I just happen to be the mayor of Hangtown. The town's rebounding nicely. The marshal and I were just discussing the imminent revival of Hangtown.'

Josh again saw a glance flicker from man to man. As he had hoped, his mention of a local law officer seemed to strike a cautionary note. He knew these men not at all, but there was a dangerous aura surrounding them.

'Let's just ride on,' the narrow man called Bert suggested. He was obviously nervous now, glancing around from shadow to shadow. A third man said, 'My pony couldn't make it to the other end of town. He's worn down to the nub.'

Jay became transparently polite. 'Mayor, if you can show us where to water and feed our horses, where we can get a meal, show us a place to sleep, we'd be appreciative.'

Josh Banks breathed a little easier. This just might play out the way he wished. 'Tell you what I can do, men, there's a little seep just beyond the town limits and grass for your horses. Food, we're awful short on, but I can let you have some venison if you feel up to roasting it over a camp-fire.' He paused, 'As to a place to sleep, I can't do a lot for you. The army contingent could arrive at any time, and we agreed to hold the hotel rooms for them. I can't let you sleep in the stable either – there's a town ordinance against that. But if you don't mind sleeping out, we can take care of you well enough.'

'It's the best we're going to get, Jay,' Bert said.

'I've been sleeping out for three weeks, one more night won't kill me,' another rider put in.

'My pony's done in.'

'Roast venison sounds fine to me,' the fourth man said.

'All right,' Jay said, his forced politeness slipping. In a more surly tone he told Josh Banks, 'We'll take you up on your offer. Show us where we can water our ponies.'

Later, while Wage Carson was at the hotel retrieving their saddle-rolls, and presumably mooning around in the kitchen with Liza, Josh was doing his best to clean up the marshal's office where he had decided it was better to stay now. By the dimmest light of dusk, he succeeded in lighting the lantern which still hung on the wall, found a broom in a small utility closet and began sweeping. In the morning he meant to repair the broken leg on the battered desk, for the sake of appearances, and poke around for keys to the jail's two cells. He had left the door open to the cool of the settling evening and was startled when the shadow of an unheard visitor fell across the buckled floor of the office. Turning, he found Cora Kellogg, still dressed in black, watching him.

'Good evening, Mayor,' she said.

'Evening,' Josh Banks said to the stout woman. 'Something I can do for you?'

'You may or may not be aware of it,' she said,

looking around the dusty room, 'but there will be some soldiers from Fort Thomas arriving in the next few days. Looking for some female companionship,' she said with an innocent smile.

'You are planning on staying that long, then?' Josh asked, holding his broom with both hands.

'I sort of agreed,' she said as if it were none of her doing. 'The trooper that passed through is an old friend of mine.'

'I see,' Josh mumbled. Then remembering his position, he added, 'We can't have those soldiers in the hotel. Town ordinance.' His voice was harsh but hoarse.

'I realize that.' Cora circled the room, started to seat herself in a wooden chair, changed her mind and said, 'That is why I've come to see you.' She smiled wearily, but with seeming good humor. 'What I had in mind – you have seen the deserted saloon, of course. I was thinking that the girls and I could clean it up a little and make a sort of dancehall out of it. I don't know what we'd do for music,' she laughed, 'but it would make a sort of social club where the boys from Fort Thomas could talk to the girls. These are lonely men, Mayor. It would mean a lot to them.'

'I don't know,' Josh said, scratching his gray-thatched head. 'It might be all right. Of course, the marshal would have to look in from time to time to make sure. . . .'

'That's all right,' Cora said, touching her breast with her fingertips. 'I assure you that my intentions are pure.'

Josh doubted that, but there was no objection he could think of. It wouldn't do to have the cavalrymen romping through the hotel. Slowly he nodded, 'I suppose it will be all right as long as things are kept under control.'

'I promise you they will be,' Cora Kellogg said emphatically. She smiled again, turned and went out into the night, leaving Josh to wonder if he had made the right decision. But even if he had not wanted to allow it, what were he and Wage to do to stop it? Frowning, he got back to his sweeping.

After leaving the marshal's office, Cora made her way across the dusty street to the stable where Gus Travers had made his bed in the back of the Conestoga wagon. There was no light to see by but the glimmer of starlight through the open doors. Cora walked to the tailgate of the wagon and called up, 'Hey, Gus!'

The old man was slow in answering, rising from a deep dreamless sleep. 'What is it, Cora?' he asked at length, peering out from the canvas flap of the wagon.

'How did that whiskey barrel ride?'

'How did. . . ?' Gus was still muzzy with sleep. He yawned. 'It's all right, Cora. I looked at it this afternoon.'

'Fine,' she replied, glancing once at the open doors behind her. 'Tomorrow I want you to roll it over to the old saloon – you'll find it. Better use the alley to get there. We're getting ready for a ball, and the boys will want some liquid hilarity.'

Wage Carson stood leaning against the wall in the large, smoky hotel kitchen. He watched Liza at her work, washing dishes, sharpening knives, scrubbing every open surface. He liked the slender curve of her back, the intense look on her face as she labored. He had offered to help, but she actually pushed him aside, telling Wage that she knew what she was doing and how she wanted everything arranged.

'Why is it that the other ladies don't help you?' he asked.

'Because it's my job,' she said, hesitating in her work long enough to turn toward him, her large dark eyes briefly challenging. Wage looked into them for a moment and then let his gaze fall away bashfully.

'How exactly did you come to be traveling with them?' Wage inquired. For him he was being bold. Women usually left him in near panic the few times he had encountered any. Liza was intimidating as well, but maybe because she was his age, he felt slightly more comfortable with her than he ever had with any other. He didn't think she was going to answer him, but she did.

Without pausing in her work, she said across her shoulder, 'My mother was a good friend of Cora's. They traveled all across the territory together for years. Not too long after I was born, Mother got sick. When I was three years old, she passed away. Cora took me in. Sometimes we lived in towns, sometimes we traveled here and there. Cora always had a few lovely girls traveling with us, dressed up in finery, but she would never allow me to get gussied up. Said that she had promised my mother that she wouldn't.'

Liza shrugged. 'I didn't really belong with them, you see, but Cora let me stay with her, and where else was I to go out here on the desert? I just decided to make myself as useful as possible to pay Cora back for all that she had done for me, and so I have.'

'I see,' Wage said, not quite sure if he really did understand. 'Well,' he said, nodding at the pile of bedding that he had brought down from his second-floor room. 'I guess I had better get over to . . . my office and see if Josh wants me for anything.'

He shouldered the two bedrolls and started for the door. Just as he reached the threshold, Liza said in a small voice, 'Thank you for coming by to talk to me,' and Wage went out of the hotel, trying unsuccessfully to suppress a broad smile.

'Are we going to be pulling out this morning, Jay?'

'Sly is saying his pony is still unfit,' Jay Champion replied. The big man was sitting cross-legged on his blanket. 'And ours aren't in much better shape. It's not smart to ride yet, Dent.'

'No, I suppose not,' Dent answered. The rising sun cast his shadow crookedly across the uneven ground where they had camped. 'But we've got to consider the soldiers. If what the old man was saying is true. . . .'

'I don't know if I believed him or not,' Jay said without rising. His dark hooded eyes remained fixed on the figure he was sketching in the sand with a twig. 'But if we keep watch, we should see the soldiers' dust before they get close to Hangtown. Even if they do come across us, how could they have gotten word out of Tucson this soon? No,' Jay said, throwing his stick into the cold fire where they had roasted their venison the night before, 'it's only smart to rest the ponies for another day.'

'I suppose,' Dent said uneasily.

Bert was awake now, walking to join them. The youngster's eyes were bright despite the long ride and heavy sleeping. 'What're we doing?' he asked.

'Staying,' Jay told him shortly.

'That's what I figured. Say, Jay, I was thinking I might walk down into town and look around if you haven't any objections.'

'What is there to see in this place?' Dent asked with a laugh, waving a hand toward the abandoned, sun-battered Hangtown.

'Nothing, I suppose.' Bert scratched his head and put his hat on. 'But if you'll forgive me, I've seen nothing but desert sand and your three faces for two weeks now. Almost anything would be of interest. Who knows,' he yawned, 'there might be something laying around that we could put to use.'

'Like rusty pickaxes?' Dent jibed.

'You never know – people leave all kinds of stuff behind when they're in a hurry to get shot of a place.'

'I don't care,' Jay said, 'do what you like. But don't get yourself in trouble with the local law. We might not be able to pull you out.'

As Dent and Jay watched, the whistling kid started walking down the hill away from the mesa toward Hangtown.

'Why'd you let him go?' Dent inquired. 'If he does get himself into trouble. . . .'

'If he does, there's one fewer man to split the take with. Which reminds me. Rouse Sly out of his blanket, and the two of you find a safe place to stash our goods. If we're going to stay around for another day or two, it wouldn't do to have it out in the open where the town marshal might run across it. I haven't ridden this far to have some small-town lawman bring us to grief.'

Bert Washburn strode down the stunted-grass slope toward Hangtown, whistling as he went, The sun was warm but not yet desert-hot, the sky clear as crystal. He was going nowhere, but glad to be going. He was weary of straddling his pony, tired of the predictable talk among Sly, Dent and Jay Champion which consisted of alternate grumbling and boasting. Once they split up the loot from that Tucson bank, Bert decided that he was going to get shot of the other three. He had needed to make a quick stake, and now he had it.

Hangtown looked no better in full sunlight than it had the evening before. Faded paint, sagging awnings, buckled plankwalks, weeds growing the length of its rutted street. It didn't matter – he was *someplace*. Bert peered in the windows of a few abandoned establishments, seeing little of interest – scattered papers, broken furniture, empty crates. The residents of the former silver town hadn't wasted any time when they had decided to abandon it.

Bert was growing thirsty. He tried a pump in the center of town where a scraggly cottonwood tree grew, and found it dry as dust. Another reason the town was deserted? He stood in the scant shade of the withered cottonwood and removed his hat to wipe his brow. There was not a horse to be seen, not a single citizen. No bird chirped, no dog barked. He considered – there had to be water somewhere. What about the hotel? If the soldiers were to be billeted there, it seemed there must be a working water pump nearby. He started that way.

The day was beginning to warm rapidly, and he moved to the plankwalks on the north side of the street, welcoming the ribbon of shade the few sagging awnings offered. He was within half a block of the hotel when he froze in his tracks, scooted into a narrow alley between two buildings and peered around the corner. A smile slowly formed itself on his lips.

There she was, crossing the street toward the boarded-up saloon opposite. A woman in yellow silk. He could not see her face. A minute later a second woman, wearing bright red followed, holding her skirts up to keep them from trailing in the dust.

'Be damned,' he muttered to himself. It figured in a way, he supposed, if the army was sending troopers here to be billeted. These women had a knack for finding cavalry camps. He decided to head back toward the shadow of the mesa where there was water to be had. He had something to tell the others now.

Starting up the alley, he nearly ran into Wage Carson.

'Morning,' the hulking baby-faced marshal said.

'Morning,' Bert responded uneasily. He was never comfortable around a man with a badge.

'You boys doing all right up there?' Wage asked. There seemed to be some emphasis on the last two words.

'We're fine,' Bert answered.

'Good. Think you boys will be riding on soon?' The question may have been asked in all innocence, but Bert took it for a suggestion from the lawman.

'Probably another day. Our ponies were pretty beat down.'

'Well, luck to you,' Wage said with apparent candor. Then he nodded and started up the alley while Bert, after watching Wage's wide back for a minute, started back toward the outlaw camp.

Wage Carson continued across the street to the saloon. Stepping up on to the plankwalk, he entered the deserted building. It came as no surprise to him to find Liza, scarf tied over her hair, sweeping up the place while two of the ladies – Rebecca and the blonde they called Madeline – walked around the saloon commenting on its dilapidated condition.

'Need some help?' Wage Carson asked. Liza looked up from her work and shrugged.

'Don't you have other duties to perform?'

'Not just now. Things are slow,' Wage said.

'Well, if you really have the time: there's a bucket and a mop over there. You could mop behind me as I sweep … if you really don't mind.'

'I don't mind,' Wage said, rolling up his

47

sleeves. 'Besides, I've nothing else to do.'

'Where've you been?' Josh Banks asked later that afternoon when Wage returned to the marshal's office, which remained cool in mid-afternoon due to its heavy walls and double ceiling designed to deter escape attempts. Wage told him and Josh nodded; he should have been able to guess. Find that little dark-haired girl and you'd find Wage nearby.

'I need you for a little while. I want you to lift up that corner of the desk while I pound a few support nails into the leg.'

'This place is starting to look like an office,' Wage said appreciatively. 'You've been busy too.'

'Not bad, is it? Considering what I had to work with.'

'Josh. . . .' Wage faltered. 'While I was walking around this morning, I met one of those strangers looking the town over.' Josh Banks's eyebrows lifted. 'And, as I was helping Liza clean the saloon up, that old man, Gus, came in the back door rolling a barrel. Josh – I'm pretty sure it was whiskey.'

'Cora is getting ready for the soldiers, it seems,' Josh said. 'Damnit, I guess she played me for a fool.'

'What do we do now, Josh?'

'First we fix this desk, then we oil the hinges on the cell doors.' Josh was thoughtful. He added, 'When you go out from now on, Wage, why don't you carry your rifle with you? Not that I think you'll need it, but when people see you carrying a long gun it puts them on notice that you might mean business.'

'You're thinking about those men camped up along the mesa?'

'I'm thinking about them, the women, the soldiers and the barrel of whiskey,' Josh Banks said. 'Come on, hoist that desk corner for me.'

FOUR

Laredo sat his big buckskin horse on the rock-strewn knoll just south of Hangtown. He had nearly lost the trail of Jay Champion and his gang of robbers, but had found it again as they emerged from the sand dune country. They could not travel long and far, not without water, not with the shape that their horses were in. They had to be holed up in or somewhere near this ghost town.

He cuffed the perspiration from his brow and studied the ramshackle town, the brooding mesa beyond it and then started on his way. His horse was in no better shape than those ridden by the Champion gang, his thirst no less.

Nearing the weather-beaten town he saw that it was not totally abandoned. A surrey sat behind the sun-blistered stable. A horse wickered. Along the rutted street the figure of a man could be seen, and farther along what appeared to be a small woman in man's clothing emerged from a building to throw out a bucket of water.

Laredo approached slowly, partly because of the weariness of his mount, partly because he had no idea who any of these people were, or whether Champion and his crew had made their base here – for all he knew Hangtown was an outlaw hideout. Asking questions in an unknown town was always risky.

Laredo knew. He had been in the business of pursuing men for a long time.

It had begun because of a man named Jake Royle. Down and out, Laredo had been eyeballing the bank in a small town called Carmel in southern Arizona. Laredo was hungry, tired and broke. While he stood considering the bank, a man who moved on cat feet slipped up beside him in hot shade of the alleyway and introduced himself.

'Jake Royle's my name,' he said, stuffing the bowl of a stubby pipe with tobacco.

'Pleased to meet you,' Laredo said shortly. He was not in the mood for idle conversation with a stranger.

'Working in town, are you?' Royle persisted, lighting his pipe.

'Not at the moment.'

Royle nodded, blew out a stream of blue smoke and studied the tall stranger. 'I, myself, am employed here,' he said. Laredo cast annoyed eyes on the stocky old-timer. 'For now, that is. I travel all around,' Royle continued, indicating all of the territory with a wave of his pipe.

'What are you, some kind of drummer?'

'No. I am employed, my young friend, as an operative in the enforcement arm of the Territorial Bank examiner's office.'

'Oh?' Laredo felt cornered suddenly. The inoffensive little man apparently had some standing. Laredo wondered how Royle could have known what he had in mind that hot, dry, desperate day.

'Yes' Royle went on, 'you know, men will try to stick up these little banks in isolated areas, and very often succeed. Then, once they have beaten the town marshal to the city limits, gotten out of the county before the sheriff can catch them, they figure they've gotten away with the job. They'll ride on to Mexico, California, anywhere, free as birds. Or so they think. The local law doesn't have the time or resources to expend hunting them down. Me,' Royle said with a gnome-like smile. 'I've got all the time in the world, son. All the time in the world.' With that the little man nodded and walked away. Laredo stood watching. If that had not been a warning, it was the next thing to one.

It wasn't until late afternoon that Laredo traced Royle to the hotel room where he sat shirtless, bare feet propped up.

'Mr Royle,' Laredo said, 'how's chances of getting hired on in a job like yours?'

Now Laredo studied the desert-defeated town of Hangtown from the cactus-stippled knoll to the south. He didn't much like the idea of riding into a potentially deadly situation, but his horse was beat-up, he was out of water, and it wouldn't be the first time he had been forced to walk into a situation blind.

Besides, up until the day of his death, Jake Royle had repeated endlessly: 'They can run, but they can not hide. Not from us.'

Laredo patted his big horse's neck and started down from the knoll.

Wary of an ambush, he rode cautiously, eyes flickering from point to point. None of the four men he was pursuing should have known him,

53

but perhaps there were others around who knew Laredo's face and profession. You never knew. Six months earlier he had been caught in a trap near Scottsdale and spent five weeks on his back recovering from the gunshots. Laredo was not eager to repeat the experience.

Unexpectedly, he found himself approaching what a faded sign declared to be the town marshal's office. So there was some sort of law here. The door was open and a gray-haired man with a beard was sweeping off the porch.

Laredo swung his faltering horse that way.

'You the marshal here?' he asked from horseback. Josh Banks shifted his eyes to the well set-up, trail-dusty stranger.

'Not me,' Josh replied. 'I'm just helping out. I'm the mayor here. Marshal's busy just now, and there's a lot to do around town.'

'I see. Well, I need water and feed for my horse. Is there a place I can stable him up?'

'Stable is being saved for the soldiers due to arrive,' Josh said cautiously. 'Other passers-by have been advised to water at the seep at the foot of the mesa.' He waved a hand toward the dark bulk of the massive landform.

'Other strangers?' Laredo asked, trying a smile. 'I wonder if I know them.'

'I wouldn't know. I heard the names Jay, Bert and Sly – mean anything to you?'

'No,' Laredo answered although he knew that he had found his men. 'I had hopes of finding some friends. Listen,' he said, leaning forward, his hands cupped on the pommel of his saddle, 'I don't much like the idea of camping out with men I don't know. Isn't there some way I can maybe sleep in the stable?'

'There's a town ordinance—' Josh began and then he saw the glint of sunlight on a ten-dollar gold piece in Laredo's hand. 'Of course, with a special permit. . . .'

'Any chance you could take care of that for me?' Laredo asked.

'Under these circumstances. I mean I wouldn't want you to have to blanket up with a bunch of men who might not mean you well. It would be sort of a protective decision – however you might phrase that. I'll take care of it, mister. The permit will run you about ten dollars, though.'

'Seems high,' Laredo said with a smile, 'but it costs money just to stay alive, doesn't it?' He flipped the gold piece toward Josh. It glittered as it spun. Josh caught it neatly in his hat.

'There's one other fellow staying over in the stable,' Josh said. 'An old man named Gus. He sleeps nights in the Conestoga wagon you'll see. He won't give you anything to worry about. It's about the time of day he takes his own horses up to the seep to water them. He'll either show you the way or might be convinced to water your buckskin for you for a dollar or two . . . if you don't care to be seen.'

Suspicion had returned to Josh Banks's eyes; what was *this* one hiding out from.

'I thank you. I'll see what Gus can do for me. What time is the marshal due back?'

'It's sort of hard to say,' Josh answered. It depended on how long Liza could put up with him.

'I'd like to talk to him,' Laredo said. 'I'll try again later.'

Then Laredo tipped his hat and turned the big buckskin horse with the splash of white on its chest and started toward the stable. Josh was left to stand on the porch holding his broom, frowning and wondering. What now?

By the time Wage Carson returned to the jail, the sun was dropping behind the mesa, extending its cooling shadow toward the town.

He found Josh Banks sitting behind the repaired desk in the jail, hands behind his head.

'Who was that man I saw over here?' Wage asked, seating himself in one of the straight-backed wooden chairs.

'I don't think he ever did give me his name,' Josh said, lowering his arms.

'Well, what did he want, then?'

'He wanted to sleep in the stable. I told him that he could.'

'I thought we had a town ordinance against that,' Wage said. He rose and placed his rifle in the disused gunrack.

'We do,' Josh answered, 'but I issued him a special permit. Here it is,' he said, moving the ten-dollar gold piece on the desk with his index finger.

'Is that the way we're going to do business around here?' Wage asked with disappointment.

'No, it isn't, son. The law is the law, this one just needs to be amended a little. The man didn't think it was safe to camp out with four rough men he doesn't know. You can understand that, can't you?'

'I suppose so,' Wage answered. 'Those men up by the seep, Josh, where do you think they're traveling to? Way out here.'

'My guess would be,' Josh said, rising, 'that they're not going to something, but away from it.

Their ponies were awfully beat up.'

'That would be my guess as well,' Wage said glumly. 'Well, there's nothing for them here. Why would they hang around?'

Both knew the answer to that. Josh asked, 'How are the ladies coming along over in the saloon?'

'Liza's the only one there. I don't know why the girl puts up with matters the way they are.'

'Did she tell you?'

'She says she has no other choice.'

'Well then?'

'Those soldiers are due in tomorrow, aren't they, Josh?'

'So I've been told. Why?'

'I don't know. In a way it makes me feel safer with those men still camping up there along the seep. In another way it gets me to worrying. I don't suppose half a dozen liquored-up soldiers will be much less trouble than four rough men on the run.'

'Let's hope they mind their manners, that Cora Kellogg keeps them in check. If not,' Josh said, glancing toward the cells, 'you might have your work cut out for you.'

'Don't I know it,' the bulky kid said gloomily. Josh approached him and said:

'We can still high-tail it, Wage. It seems I've

gotten you into something a little over your head.'

'You didn't get me into anything, Josh. A man makes his own choices. But the answer is "no", I don't want to leave. It doesn't do for a marshal to run out on his own town. It'd be plain cowardly.'

And there was Liza to consider. She might need some protection and he was the only one who could provide it for her.

Josh could read the young man's mind. He wasn't sure that Wage was being wise, but a man has to have his pride – if he is to be called a man at all. Josh Banks had commandeered the cot in the marshal's front office. There he had spread out his bedroll and he went to it now, turning the lamp down in passing. It was early yet, but he was getting to be an old man and his bones sometimes ached. Pulling off his boots, he wrapped a blanket around himself. Wage Carson remained sitting in the near-darkness for a long time, trying to solve a problem for which there seemed to be no answer.

It was still early in the morning, the sun just breaking the eastern horizon when Bert Washburn, rising early from his blankets, saw the dust far out on the white-sand desert. Squinting into the harsh dawn light he tried to make out the incoming riders, but could not. He walked to where Jay Champion was sleeping. Bert crouched and shook the outlaw leader's shoulder.

Jay sat up in a flash, drawing his Colt as he rose.

'Oh, it's you. What do you want?' the black-bearded man asked angrily.

'There's men riding this way, Jay,' Bert told him. 'I figured we might have to get ready to ride.'

Sly had also awakened, and the narrow gunman rose to his feet in one catlike motion. None of them – except Dent – ever slept heavily. Doing so could spell the end for men on the run. Jay Champion was on his feet as well now. He peered into the sunlight with sleep-reddened eyes, watching the dark approaching figures of horsemen.

Virgil Sly said, 'Isn't this the day the soldiers were supposed to arrive? Maybe it's them.'

'There's only five, six of them,' Jay said. 'Not much of a cavalry contingent if they're expecting Indian raids in the area.'

'I've been thinking about that,' Bert Washburn said. Now Dent had crawled from his bed to join them. 'I don't think they're being billeted here at all. Remember I told you that I saw two women in town? Well, they weren't dressed like no miners' wives. And it seems to me – without a calendar – that we're close to army payday. No sir, I think that desert rat who called himself the mayor of Hangtown, whoever he was, was flat-out lying to us.'

'I don't get you, Bert,' Dent said. He looked haggard, ready to flee at any moment.

'I think, Dent, that what we have here is a band of fancy ladies waiting for a bunch of cavalrymen with a three-day pass and their pockets filled with government pay.'

'But the mayor—' Sly began.

'Mayor of what? Hangtown! It's enough to make you laugh, isn't it, Sly? No, the "mayor" is traveling with the ladies, I'd bet, and he was just trying to keep us out of town until the pony soldiers got here.'

'I think you're right,' Jay Champion said, scowling. 'What does this ramshackle town need a mayor and a marshal for? Why didn't they want us to sleep in the stable under a decent roof?'

'Another man was sacked-out there last night,' Bert said. His interest in the activities in and around Hangtown was unabated. 'I saw him.'

'What did he look like?' Jay asked, his scowl deepening.

Bert gave the best description of Laredo that he could. Jay shook his head. 'That doesn't remind me of anyone I know. Still, let's keep an eye on him. Could be the law, though I don't know why they'd send one man after us instead of a posse. I think, boys, we'd better keep our horses ready to ride from now on.'

The cavalrymen drew nearer. The shadows of early morning withdrew and now they could see that they were definitely soldiers in their blues. And that there were six of them only. Bert jabbed a finger toward the town and they watched as three women in silk dresses emerged from the hotel to welcome the incoming men.

'Be damned,' Dent muttered. 'It looks like you were right, Bert.' Jay was meditative. 'Where did you stash the money, Sly?'

'In the old mine shaft over there. It's safe. There's a little ledge about head high. We put the saddle-bags in there and hid them with a few rocks.'

'That should do it. We'll leave it there for now. I don't like riding out past the soldiers. But they won't be here long. When their pay is gone, they'll leave. And when the soldiers are gone, the women will leave. We'll wait them out for a few more days.'

'There's still the marshal,' Bert put in.

'What's he look like? The dangerous sort?'

'He's a chunky kid, looks like a big farm boy. Not much to worry about.'

'Fine. He won't be chasing us out of here. We stay, let our ponies get well-rested. When the soldiers are gone, we go.'

'That means we're going to need some more supplies,' Sly said. 'We cleaned that venison to the bone last night.'

'We'll find a way to replenish,' Jay said, waving an indifferent hand. The soldiers wouldn't want to go hungry, nor would the women. There were supplies to be had in Hangtown, had to be.

They watched now as the soldiers trailed into town, some whistling, waving their hats in the air, in a celebratory mood. One of them tried to sweep a woman up from horseback. It looked as if the party was on.

Jay's restlessly shifting gaze watched as the tall man at the other end of the street emerged from the stable to watch the activity, hands on hips. Who was he? Jay Champion figured he had things well in hand; he didn't like the idea of there being a wild card in the deck.

'The marshal already knows you, Bert. Why don't you go back down there, and see if you can find some supplies. And,' he added, 'see if you can get a handle on who that stranger is.'

Bert agreed eagerly, taking his assignment as a sign of trust. The truth was that the other three outlaws had already decided among themselves that the naïve Bert Washburn was expendable. If he ran into trouble, well, then that was his misfortune and none of their own.

Bert made his way down the short grass hill once again, entering the town through the alley he had used on his last visit to Hangtown. In the heated shade of the narrow alleyway he paused to rest for a minute, trying to decide what to do first. He had been given two chores: find provisions; try to discover who the tall stranger was. If he happened to run into the baby-faced marshal again, he could strike up a casual conversation about the newcomer, pretending that he thought he might be a friend of his. Failing that, he saw no way to achieve that goal.

The other task should be the easier. Now, from the saloon across the street he heard banjo music, heard the whoops of the soldiers, a woman's high-pitched shriek of amusement, He glanced at the soldiers' bay horses, lined along the hitch rail and pondered. If virtually everyone in town was in the saloon, why then there was no one in the hotel.

That was the obvious place to look for food, wasn't it? The women had to have been eating. If the soldiers had been expected, there must be something for them as well.

Bert Washburn returned to the back of the building and sidled toward the hotel. The rear door was ajar. Beyond it was a kitchen. Bert smiled. This was going to be easy. Take whatever food he could find, stash it and then go about trying to discover the identity of the strange rider.

Cautiously Bert slipped inside the kitchen, and two things happened at once.

He saw a small dark-haired girl in men's clothing scrubbing the kitchen down, and at the outer door a blond cavalryman slipping into the kitchen, his eyes fixed on the girl. The soldier had a wolfish look on his face, and he stepped toward the little girl. He meant her no good. Halfway there he noticed Bert and spun toward him. The young soldier pawed at the flap of his cavalry holster, but Bert's holster carried no such impediment and he drew and shot the soldier in the chest.

The girl screamed, the soldier sagged against the wall and slid to the floor. Bert took to his heels and sprinted toward the mesa.

In the marshal's office, Wage Carson jumped to

his feet as the pistol shot echoed through the narrow street. Josh Banks went to the door and swung it open to the white sunlight of the desert morning. Soldiers, guns in hands, were swarming toward the hotel, women in bright silk dresses watching them as they charged across the overgrown street.

'What in hell is happening?' Wage Carson asked Josh.

'Son, it seems that civilization has returned to Hangtown.'

FIVE

Liza sat in one of the wooden chairs in the office, explaining what she had seen to Josh and Wage Carson. She was not tearful or hysterical, but certainly she was shaken by the shooting.

'One of the soldiers – I don't even know his name – stopped me earlier on the street and tried to paw me. I shrugged him off and went in to get on with my work. He called after me that he would catch up with me later. Well, I guess that was what he had in mind – in a world where every woman is available, one that isn't is never safe.

'I was finishing scrubbing down the stove. Since I had used it for roasting venison, it was pretty well spattered. I sensed, more than heard him come in. It was the same soldier, with a . . . more than eager look in his eyes. As I half-turned

67

toward him, wondering if I could reach a frying pan to bonk his skull with, another man I had never seen before, in civilian clothes, who was a quicker draw, shot the cavalryman dead as he tried to reach his sidearm. Then that man ran away. That's about it,' she said, sniffling a little now, blotting at her nose with a small handkerchief.

Wage Carson, whose entire law enforcement career consisted of walking up and down the streets of Hangtown for the last few days, was unsure how to proceed. Josh Banks helped him out.

'What did the man who did the shooting look like, Liza?'

'It all happened so fast,' she said shaking her head, but she gave them a vague description of Bert Washburn. Wage frowned, thinking that it might have been the man he had seen the day previous. There were so few men around Hangtown that could have done it, that it seemed nearly a certainty that it was one of the crowd camped at the seep. However, he was not sure of one point:

'Josh, it don't seem to me that a crime was committed. The man was protecting Liza. Isn't that the same as self-defense?'

'I judge so,' Josh answered, although he had nothing to base his words on. Of course there was the question of what the shooter had been doing in the hotel. It could have been that he wanted nothing more than a drink of water. Or. . . .

Josh said, 'I'm sure not going to tell you to go up and arrest this fellow. Even if we had a mind to, it would be you against four armed and presumably dangerous men. What I think is that now we should just set a goal of making sure that there aren't any more incidents like this.'

'Need any help, then?' a new voice asked, and all eyes were drawn to the tall stranger who stood in the doorway, silhouetted against the glare of afternoon light. Laredo stepped into the office, removing his hat.

'Don't mean to interrupt,' he said with a nod toward Liza, 'but I was wandering over to see what was happening uptown and I happened to hear you talking. Seems like the marshal here might be a little outnumbered just now. Nine men with guns and just him to keep them quiet. I thought I'd volunteer my help.'

'Are you an experienced lawman?' Wage asked hopefully.

'I've done some work in that line,' Laredo told him.

'Josh?' Wage asked hopefully.

'I don't know – we haven't the money in the town budget to pay a deputy,' Josh told Laredo.

'I'd be happy to do it as a civic duty,' the tall man said. 'For the time being,' he added with a smile.

'I just don't know—' Josh said in real confusion.

Wage interrupted him. 'We'd better do something and quick, Josh. The soldiers are gathered in front of the saloon, and they are stirred up. It looks like they're thinking of taking care of matters themselves.'

'We can't have that!' Josh said, a little shaken now. 'Besides, if these troopers try to rush that camp up there – well, those men have a rough look about them. I'm not all that sure that the soldiers would come out on the winning end.'

'Let's talk to them now,' Laredo suggested. 'All three of us before they get themselves worked up any further.'

Josh liked none of it, but he dug a badge out of the desk, tossed it to Laredo, planted his battered hat on his head and went out, following the stranger and Wage, who was carrying his Winchester. Halfway along the street the soldiers caught sight of them and turned to watch with challenging eyes.

'I've got to get to Cora, tell her what happened,' Josh said. 'I'm going around the back way. You two hold these men until we can talk reasonably to them.'

Wage nodded dully. He had never been in a situation like this before and they were outnumbered five to two. The tall man who had introduced himself as Laredo seemed unconcerned, as if this were a daily occurrence in his world.

'They're hopping mad,' Wage said in a whisper.

'Sure they are. A friend of theirs just got murdered – or so they believe. Maybe the mayor and this Cora can explain it well enough to satisfy them.' Stepping up on to the boardwalk Wage and Laredo walked the length of it until they were only a few feet away from the angry knot of soldiers.

'What's all this?' one of the soldiers asked, seeing the badges on the two.

'Just trying to stop trouble before it begins,' Laredo said smoothly.

'It's already begun,' the soldier said defiantly.

'Yes, it has. We're only asking you not to make it any worse until you know the whole story.' The military instinct in the men urged them to fight

71

back and rush after the man they saw as the killer of their friend. Probably they did not even know that there were four hard cases up there who would undoubtedly be waiting for them by now.

'Step inside for a while, boys,' Laredo said. 'Maybe we can straighten this out. If not, you've lost only a few minutes.'

'Osborne!' A voice Wage easily identified as Cora Kellogg's called from inside the smoky saloon. 'Dan! You all come in here for a few minutes. I know what really happened.'

Grousing, cursing, the troopers followed Corporal Osborne's lead and tramped into the lighted saloon. The two other women – Rebecca and the blonde Madeline – sat on a bench in the corner, close together, hands between their knees, The whiskey barrel sat prominently on the bar, Old Gus Travers, banjo in his hands, sipped at something out of a chipped ceramic cup. Cora marched to the center of the room as the soldiers formed themselves into a half-circle.

'Boys, listen to me. You know that little girl that travels with me – Liza – well, it seems that your friend . . . what was his name?'

'Coleman!' a couple of them shouted in angry unison.

'Coleman, then, followed Liza into the hotel.

Maybe he has no head for whiskey, I don't know. But he tried some rough stuff with her. The second man, the one who shot Coleman, happened upon them and Coleman drew. The other gent shot him. That's the way it happened, and that's all that should happen. You have my word for that. You might have liked this Coleman, maybe he was a good man otherwise, but he was totally at fault on this day.

'I recommend you put your guns down, forget about tracking down an innocent man, raise a glass and dance with the girls.'

There was a moment or two of quiet debate, but eventually Corporal Osborne shrugged and said. 'If Cora says it's so, boys, it's true. I know her well enough. Poor Coleman, but if he was in the wrong . . . let's get back to dancing.'

Some of the troopers were reluctant to give up the idea, others seemed just as pleased to forget the fight. Josh Banks said a hurried goodbye, but Laredo told Wage, 'I think maybe we should hang around outside in case they change their minds. Liquor can do that.'

The two retreated to the boardwalk and took up seats on the wooden bench there as evening settled. Gus started his banjo-playing again while the soldiers whooped and danced inexpertly with

Rebecca, Madeline and Cora. The desert began to grow cool. The banjo started to get on Wage's nerves. It seemed the old man knew only 'Greensleeves,' 'Dixie' and 'Red River Valley', which he played until it became nerve jangling. After a while the chords became mixed up until it was difficult at times to tell what song Gus was searching for on his strings. Probably the old man was tippling a lot of whiskey himself.

'That's enough of this for me,' Wage said as an hour and then another rolled by and the cavalrymen showed no sign of returning to their hunt. He rose stiffly and looked toward the bulk of the mesa. 'Do you think we ought to go up and tell them that things have been smoothed out?'

'No,' Laredo said with a smile. 'I can't say much in favor of that idea. Two lawmen walking into an armed camp in the dark? No.'

'That's what I was hoping you'd say,' Wage answered. 'Thanks for your help. For me, I've got to catch some sleep.'

'All right,' Laredo said cheerfully. 'See you in the morning.'

'You're coming back?' Wage frowned. 'You don't think this is over yet, do you?'

'Marshal,' Laredo had to tell him, 'I don't think it's even begun.'

'That was a damned fool stunt,' Jay Champion growled at Bert Washburn. Together with Sly they were crouched around the embers of their dying campfire. Dent was out watching the town for signs of approach.

'I'm telling you, Jay,' Bert protested, 'the soldier was drawing on me. There wasn't any other choice.'

'The question is, what do we do now?' Sly said, his black eyes fixed as if fascinated on the red-gold embers in the fire ring. 'Because if we ride out, who's to say that the soldiers might not take a notion to ride on our heels and settle accounts?'

'How can we stay here?' Bert asked with deep trepidation, having no way of knowing what had transpired in town after his hasty departure.

Jay Champion held up two hands and bent one finger down. 'It's only five of them against the four of us,' he said smugly. 'Don't you think we could take them in a fight?'

'There's the law,' Bert said, still nervous. His instinct was to bolt out on to the desert before someone could find a tree to hang him from. His dream of providing himself with a stake to start a small ranch was threatened. The Tucson bank job had gone smoothly enough, if you didn't consider the dead teller, and he planned on getting shot of the gang at the first opportunity after the loot was split. This, he had decided, was not the life for him. They treated him fairly for the most part, but at times he had suspicions that they would as soon double-cross him and divide his share. It seemed, at this moment, that Jay and the others were willing enough to remain in Hangtown and let Bert be strung up, if that was what it took to ensure their own safety.

'The law?' Jay smirked. 'What did you tell me that was here? One big farm boy. Do you think he's going to interfere?'

'No,' Bert answered, mentally reviewing what he knew of Wage Carson. 'I wouldn't want to get into a wrestling match with the big kid, but as far as gunplay – no.'

'Well then . . . what do you think Sly?' Jay Champion asked his long-time partner.

'I'm looking at it a little differently,' the gunfighter said, lifting his eyes from the dead fire. 'We can't take a chance on leaving just now, because those troopers might take a notion to ride us down out on the desert. If they decided on that, they'd find the money on us as well. We'd end up dead and broke at once.'

'So then?' Champion asked.

'Only this – suppose they have no way of

following us? I say we take their ponies.'

Jay Champion actually smiled, his thick lips curling fractionally upward behind his black beard.

'It's a thought. Can it be done?'

Sly rose from his crouch and stretched his back. 'Jay, you know as well as I do that anything can be done if there's enough reason to do so and a man has the heart for it.'

'Go get Dent,' Jay told Bert, who scrambled up and started toward the head of the trail to town. 'When do you think we ought to try it?' Champion asked Sly.

'By midnight those soldier boys will be good and liquored up. They started early,' the gunman answered. 'When we see the lights go out in the saloon, we give it an hour and then make our way down.'

'What if they have a guard posted?'

Virgil Sly shrugged as if it were of no importance. 'We tell him that the marshal sent us over to take their horses to the stable.'

'It sounds all right,' Jay said, frowning with his eyebrows, 'but there's a deal of risk to it.'

Sly almost laughed out loud. 'Isn't there? But, Jay, tell me how many risks we've run in the last five years.'

Jay Champion answered with another of his infrequent smiles and nodded his shaggy head. 'All right. It's either that or we shoot it out with them.' Dent and Bert had returned and now the outlaws settled in to refine the plan.

It was decided that Sly, Jay Champion and Dent would ride into town in the dead of night and collect the army horses, lead them out on to the desert and remove their bridles and saddles. Bert would be left behind near the mesa to stand watch over the stolen money that was hidden in the mine shaft. His signal to ride to meet them would be a single shot they would fire to scatter the army horses, leaving the troopers afoot.

If, on the other hand, Bert spotted the soldiers or the law trying to approach the camp, he was to fire two shots to summon the others back. Then, they all knew, it would become a real shooting war. Mounted, sober, more experienced at this kind of work, against nearly equal numbers of men, the outlaws felt that they would still have the advantage, although they hoped things would not get that far.

'Well, Bert,' Jay Champion said sourly. 'You started this. Are you ready to finish it now?'

Bert nodded mutely. The other men had been through dozens of shoot-outs. He had seen only one – the bank job in Tucson where he had done little more than hold the horses. But he supposed he was ready. He took a deep breath and slowly let it out. After all, without the money he was back where he had started six months earlier – except that he was now a wanted man.

'I'm ready.'

In Hangtown the soldiers had tired of their activity and nearly had it with the whiskey. They were trying their best to cut one girl or the other out of the herd before falling off to sleep. In the jail Wage Carson slept deeply on a bunk in one of the cells, his guileless face at peace. Josh Banks who had gone to bed early, was now awake, sitting on the edge of the cot in the outer office, stoking up his stubby pipe until it glowed like a distant red star in the darkness.

Liza slept in her hotel room where she had propped a chair under the doorknob. She had lain awake for hours, wondering how many more episodes like today's would befall her if she didn't find a way to break free of Cora Kellogg's party, wondering what she could possibly do if she was not working for Cora. She had no family, no trade, no money. For a little while before she slept – or perhaps she was already half-dreaming – she thought of the comforting presence of the bearlike young marshal who had befriended her, and she wondered. . . .

Laredo had his big buckskin horse saddled. His eyes were weary and dry, but he had no intention of sleeping on this night. There were half a dozen drunken soldiers in town. One of them had already tried to attack a young girl. The other five might again take the notion to avenge his death. He was certain now that the men camped near the seep were the Jay Champion gang, and they might be considering stealing away in the dead of night to avoid the soldiers. Laredo did not feel like tracking them for another hundred miles across the long desert. He wanted it ended now. He only wanted them to make one mistake.

It was still one man against four – Laredo had no intention of drawing the well-intentioned but utterly inexperienced town marshal into the fray. When he could, he tried not to lean on local law enforcement for help. It was his job, and if he could not handle it, then he ought to find another line of work.

He was sitting cross-legged on the floor of the stable, near the open double doors, counting stars. Waiting and watching. There was trouble in the air, It was nearly palpable, He began to stiffen, and his eyelids had begun to close, and so he rose, went outside and breathed in deeply, bending from side to side to try to encourage his blood to circulate. Behind him he heard someone entering the rear of the stable, and he automatically crouched and drew his revolver, but it took only a split-second to recognize the shadowy figure as the returning Gus Travers, weaving toward the Conestoga wagon, his banjo in hand. There had to be a story behind the old man's reason for traveling with Cora and the girls, but it would remain a mystery to Laredo.

We all had secrets on our backtrails that were better left undiscovered.

Gus clambered up with a groan and the clatter of his banjo against the bed of the wagon was a terrific dissonant twang. Within ten minutes, Gus could be heard softly snoring. The rest of Hangtown, the rest of the universe, had fallen into midnight silence.

Corporal Dan Osborne stood in front of the saloon feeling as low as he had in a long time. The Hangtown excursion had not gone well at all. Maybe he was too old for this. In his youthful years – not that far behind him – whiskey, women and friends had always been a formula for merriment. On this cold, lonely desert night nothing had worked.

Coleman was dead. Someone – he, himself – would have to try to explain matters to the colonel when they returned to Fort Thomas. As for the women – there were only three of them and five troopers. Osborne was one of the odd men out.

As for the whiskey, he wondered how he could ever have liked it. It was raw, burning stuff, and it had turned his stomach so that he had to retreat to the alley to throw it back up. They had had no food at all. He had assumed that there would be provisions in Hangtown. Perhaps that was why he had gotten sick, eating nothing all day. The stars seemed to blur in front of his half-drunk eyes. Hangtown was asleep. It was eerily silent. Even the breeze had died down. The huge bulk of the mesa brooded beyond. Not a dog, a skulking coyote, a rabbit, a night bird stirred. It was a hell of a vacation. He patted his pocket and realized that he had used up most of his month's pay already. On what! He recalled giving some of it to Madeline for no reason except intoxicated generosity. Perhaps he had been trying to pay for favors, but he had not phrased it that way, and she had made him no promises.

It was a damnably cold, dark and dissolute night.

Then the trio of horsemen arrived from the east end of town, slowly walking their ponies toward the saloon. Osborne unfastened the snap on his holster and pressed himself back into the shadows.

What in hell. . . ?

As he watched, the dark riders approached the rail where the six army horses still stood, and one man slipped from his saddle and began untying them while the other two looked up and down the street, at the saloon. Osborne stepped forward, pistol drawn. He shouted out, 'Just what do you think you're up to!'

And Virgil Sly shot him dead.

SIX

Laredo was into leather before the echo of the shot had died away. He touched spurs to the buckskin's flanks and raced the length of the street. He was only a few seconds too late. He saw the backs of three men as they hied the army horses out on to the desert, running their ponies at full speed. Several soldiers had come out on to the porch of the saloon. Half-dressed, their senses blurred with drink they could do nothing but stand there and mutter curses as their horses were taken. One of their company was lying flat on the boards of the walkway, quite dead.

Darkness swallowed up the men Laredo was pursuing. The long desert was pitch black. He could see a thin veil of settling dust ahead of him, and continued on, riding by guesswork. After a mile or so he could no longer see the dust or smell it as it settled earthward. Either they had outdistanced him, which seemed unlikely, or they had stopped. Laredo drew his Winchester from its saddle scabbard and went on, slowing the big buckskin to a walk, wary now of an ambush.

Star shadows laced the sand beneath a stand of tall, thorny mesquite shrubs. There was no wind. The only sounds were the creaking of leather and his own horse's clopping hoofs, though these were barely audible even to Laredo on this soft surface.

Where were they headed? Nowhere, he decided. They had not stolen the horses for profit. Ponies wearing the US brand could not be easily disposed of anyway. No, they had it in mind only to scatter the horses to keep the soldiers out of the game.

And what was their game? Simply to ride away from Hangtown. There were only three of them, though. That meant that a fourth had been left behind – unless they had decided to cut one man. out. It was a little puzzling, and Laredo let it go. He continued on aimlessly. He was basing his chosen direction on common sense – these men had no reason to zig-zag, to attempt to lose their pursuit. They would ride in a straight line, scatter the horses and then continue on. He held to the course he had been following, using the stars as his guide.

He heard the sound of hoofbeats and he halted his buckskin, cocking his rifle. The horse came out of the darkness, wide-eyed and confused. Laredo smiled thinly and lowered his rifle. It was one of the army ponies, saddleless, running in a random direction. They could not be far ahead, then, and they had stopped now to slip the bits and shed the saddles from the rest of the stolen ponies.

He walked his horse forward. He heard a muffled thump, a muted curse, and he tensed. It would have to be on foot, he decided, if he were to have a chance of slipping up on the Champion gang, and so, reluctantly, he slid from the buckskin's back and left it ground-hitched as he crept ahead, his boots whispering against the desert sand.

Five minutes later he came upon them. The three were still working at their task. No one saw him approaching in the darkness. Or so he believed. As if by instinct one of them – Sly – turned and looked directly at Laredo.

'Look out!' Sly warned, and he drew his Colt. The gunman was quick, but at that distance in the darkness, he was not that accurate. The bullet spun past Laredo's head and sang off into the distance. The other two had no thought of making a fight of it under those conditions and they leaped to their ponies' backs and spurred away on the run. Laredo levered three rounds through his Winchester, but he did not think he had tagged flesh either.

Now he was cursing himself for the decision to leave his horse behind. One of the army horses, however, was still saddled and Laredo managed to catch up its reins. The horse, used to fighting, had not been spooked by the gunshots.

Ahead of him now, Laredo saw the last of the three outlaws disappear from sight. There was a crooked, rocky arroyo up there, and the badmen had chosen to take refuge there. Laredo spurred the army bay which was willing, but had nowhere near the speed that his own buckskin possessed.

Laredo reached the rim of the arroyo which was just deep enough to conceal a mounted man, and he eased the army horse down the rocky bank. Reaching the bottom he again touched spurs to the horse and leaned low across the withers, urging the bay on. Amazingly he seemed to be gaining ground on the outlaws, for he saw two men just rounding a bend in the arroyo. He raced on for a moment before he realized his mistake.

Two men?

Where was the third? He yanked the horse's head hard to the left and ducked low as the outlaw fired at him from concealment. It saved Laredo's own life, but meant the end for the army bay who took the bullet behind his front shoulder and went down with an awkward lurch. Laredo kicked free of the stirrups and leaped from the saddle before the horse could roll on him. He hit the ground hard. The rifle was jolted from his hand and the breath was driven out of him. A second shot was fired in the night as Laredo dragged himself to the cover of a clump of stunted willow brush. Then three or four more apparently randomly-fired bullets were loosed into the darkness.

Then the night was utterly silent again. Crouched with his pistol in his hand, Laredo squinted into the darkness as if by looking hard enough he could see better, His hat had fallen off and his hair was in his eyes. His back and chest were soaked with perspiration. Nothing moved. He decided that they were probably trying to encircle him.

'Hey, Laredo!' someone called out. 'Are you all right?'

Recognizing the voice, Laredo relaxed enough to smile. 'Is it all clear?' he called back.

'Far as I can tell,' Wage Carson answered. 'I got this one. The other two never stopped or even slowed down.'

Laredo walked to where Wage was standing on the sandy bluff and took a moment to crouch beside the dead man and flick a match to life with his thumbnail.

'Do you recognize him?' Wage asked.

'Yes,' Laredo said, rising. 'A man named Broderick Dent out of Tennessee with a stop-over in Fort Leavenworth Federal Prison.'

Laredo retrieved his rifle and hat, stepped past the dead horse and scrambled up the rocky face of the bluff to find Wage sitting on his gray horse, rifle in hand.

'What are you doing out here?' Laredo asked.

'Doing my job, deputy,' Wage said, flashing one of his boyish grins. 'Climb aboard, I'll take you back to your horse.'

'Did you see which way they went?' Laredo asked.

'Not in the direction I would have expected,' Wage answered, as Laredo swung up behind him. 'They're headed straight back toward Hangtown. I might have tried to follow them, but then I heard the shot and knew they had tried to set an ambush for you.'

'It just about worked,' Laredo said. 'I sure am glad you're conscientious about your job.'

They further discussed matters after Laredo had recovered his buckskin. Wage was still puzzled, 'I don't see why they'd head back to Hangtown after committing murder there.'

'Simple. They didn't have the money with them. That's what the fourth man was doing – guarding it.'

'Money?' Wage's confusion deepened. 'I think there's a few things you haven't told me, deputy.'

Laredo enlightened him along the trail. Wage listened thoughtfully. 'You might have told me sooner,' he said, when Laredo had finished telling him about the four men and the bank hold-up in Tucson.

'I didn't see the need for it. They were bound to continue on their way in a day or two. I meant to take care of business out on the desert – at a place of my own choosing.'

'We could have rounded them up at the seep,' Wage suggested.

'When? No, Wage, things never worked out for us to have a chance at them. Besides Virgil Sly is hell on wheels with a gun and Jay Champion is as mean as they come. There would have been blood spilled. I couldn't risk having Hangtown lose its marshal in what was my fight.'

'So what will they do now? Collect their loot and ride off again?'

'I don't see that they have any other choice, do you? If there was a sober soldier in town I might consider taking some of them up there to help out. But there isn't one, and besides, who am I to give orders to an army unit – and maybe get another of them killed?'

'So what do we do now, Laredo?'

'What we can, Wage. We just do what we can.'

Bert Washburn was getting more than a little nervous. Earlier there had been a single shot, but Jay and the others could not possibly have had time to complete their mission when it sounded. They had had to fight their way out of Hangtown, it seemed. Later there had been other shots – far distant, but these could not have been signal shots either. He could think of nothing to do.

After the first shot he had seen someone he thought was the tall stranger, racing his horse the length of the street, and later still the big marshal who was unmistakable even in the dark and at this distance because of his bulk.

At the same time he had seen a body of men, the soldiers, obviously, emerge from the saloon. Bert wondered what he should do now. Jay Champion had given him his instructions, but he had not been told what to do if everything fell apart. All he could think of doing was to remain in place and guard the loot. Of course he could have just grabbed the saddle-bags and taken off on his own.

If he felt like committing suicide.

In silent desperation, Bert hunkered down behind a boulder and waited.

'All right,' PFC Cherry was saying inside the saloon, 'maybe when Coleman was shot over that girl he was in the wrong, but now they've gunned down Dan Osborne.' Cherry was a big man with a ruddy complexion. Just now his face was nearly the color of his name. He was holding forth to the gathered soldiers, some of whom were trying to dress as they listened.

'Not only that,' a soldier named Boggs put in, 'they stole our horses. Anyone feel like walking back to Fort Thomas and trying to explain to the colonel how we let that happen?'

'That's what I mean,' Cherry said. 'We got talked out of fighting before. Now, there's no other choice.'

'Who is there to fight with us on foot?' a slender private named Lassiter asked.

'There's horses in the stable,' someone suggested.

'No saddle horses,' Cherry replied as if the soldier were a fool.

'Maybe there's still some of the raiders in that camp up along the mesa,' Boggs suggested.

'Could be,' Cherry said, stroking his jaw. 'And maybe they've left some horses behind as well.'

'Makes no sense to me,' Lassiter dissented. 'Going up to an armed camp when we know that the men with our horses, the ones who killed Dan, are far out on the desert by now.'

Cora, Rebecca and Madeline were wide awake now, but Cora made no attempt to interfere this time. She knew the soldiers felt justified in wanting to fight and there would be no stopping them. Besides, she was as bitter at Dan Osborne's shooting as any of them. Dan was a little wild, but he had been a friend for many years. The other two women only stared blankly, red-eyed, at the knot of grumbling soldiers. More fun with liquored-up men! Both were wondering how they had gotten into this line of work and why they continued. Nothing but shooting, brawling, drinking and mauling. No matter where they wandered it was the same.

Cherry said, 'We can at least take a look, men. It beats sitting here doing nothing at all.'

That struck them all as logical, and so in various stages of undress and different levels of sobriety, they determined to approach the outlaw camp.

In the gloom of the mesa's shadow, Bert watched as the soldiers boiled out of the saloon. It didn't take many brains to know where they were headed. Bert still had his horse, and by leaving now he could be long gone before they reached him. Otherwise he was risking either a hanging or being shot down where he stood. He thought of the hidden bank loot again, but decided that finding it in the night, concealed as it was in a pitch-black mine shaft, he would just be wasting time when he should be fleeing. Besides, no one who was not a member of their gang was ever going to stumble across the hiding place.

He sprinted for his pony, tightened its cinches with fumbling fingers and spurred away toward the west.

'Now what?' Sly asked. The Texas gunman was breathless as they finally slowed their hard-running horses and approached Hangtown once more.

'We gather up the loot anad get the hell out of here,' Jay Champion said.

'We might have to fight our way in,' Virgil Sly said, 'and fight our way out again.'

'We might at that,' Jay replied as if that were obvious. 'If we can do it quick enough, the soldiers will see nothing but our horses' dust.'

'What about those two behind us?'

'Dent might have gotten the tall man. He was laying for him.'

'He might not have. There was more than one shot.'

Jay Champion shrugged. 'He might not have. Let's keep moving.'

Jay wasn't particularly concerned about Dent one way or the other. If the Tennesseean had been careless and gotten himself killed, that was one fewer way the money had to be split. They were nearly on top of Hangtown now. Various dim lanterns burned across the dead town. Jay automatically catalogued them: marshal's office, stable, saloon and hotel were all alight.

Slowing their horses to a walk, Sly commented, 'I don't hear any shooting, Jay. Bert should be firing if the soldiers had it in mind to charge the camp.'

'Unless he rabbited,' Jay said sourly.

'Would he take the money?'

'Not unless he's dumber than I thought,' Jay Champion muttered. 'Come on, Sly, we've got to find out what's happened sooner or later, and I don't want it to be in broad daylight.'

Standing at her upstairs hotel room window, Liza shivered in her light chemise as the night-time desert temperature plummeted. At the sound of the shot that had killed Dan Osborne, she had sprung from her bed, heart racing. From her window she had a view of the street, and she saw the raiders hieing the army horses away. Seconds later, it seemed, the deputy marshal was on their heels, then after another few minutes, as the soldiers milled and cursed on the saloon porch, she saw Wage Carson driving his gray horse the length of the street, in pursuit. Her heart sank as she watched him disappear into the night.

Maybe he wasn't much of a man as far as handsomeness went, that thick-shouldered marshal, but she knew him as kind, shy and generous, so different from the men she ran across in Cora Kellogg's employ. She had to admit it, she was drawn to his simple goodness.

And she thought that her heart would die if he were to be shot down.

Across that terrain in full darkness it was dangerous to ride at speed, but Bert Washburn was in a hurry to put distance between himself and the onrushing soldiers, and so he pushed his pony on at a pace that was on the borderline of hazardous. The horse was nimble enough, but it could see no better in the darkness than Bert could and he felt the animal's jarring misstep under him, heard a cracking sound, and the horse went down. He did not know if the horse had stepped in a squirrel hole or stumbled over a rock, but it was halted with a broken foreleg and Bert was afoot before he had even reached Hangtown.

Cursing, he staggered on down the rocky slope. He did not take the time to put the horse down; a shot would have brought the soldiers on the run. Nor did he pause mentally to pity the animal. There was blind panic riding him now and Bert meant to get away out on to the desert no matter what it took.

Reaching Hangtown, he looked up and down the street. He was now hatless, carrying his pistol in his right hand. He needed a horse, and the only possibility was the stable. He started that way, moving in a low trot through the deep shadows.

There was a lantern lit, burning low, in the stable and he searched the stalls frantically. All of the horses were dray animals, used to pulling coach or wagon, but unsuitable for riding. Cursing again, growing still more frantic, Bert considered taking one of these animals anyway.

Then he spotted, standing in the farthest stall, a white-eared mule. There was a saddle thrown over the stall partition, and a bridle hanging from a nail on the wall. With a faint smile, Bert started that way, hope building.

The mule only blinked at him dully and did not pull away from his hand as he reached for the docile animal.

'I wouldn't do that was I you,' the dry voice said from behind him. Bert froze. He still had his pistol in his hand and there was a wild determination in his eyes now. He spun, crouched, loosed off two rapid shots from his Colt in the direction of the voice, but he missed with both bullets.

Josh Banks did not miss with his rifle and Bert Washburn staggered back to collapse nearly at the feet of Josh's mule, his mouth moving soundlessly as he died.

SEVEN

'The pony soldiers are up at the camp,' Virgil Sly said as he and Jay Champion drew their horses up within sight of the seep where they had been staying. 'Why isn't Bert firing at them? Think they got him?'

'I think he rabbited,' Jay said, scowling.

'Think he took the money?'

'I don't know,' Jay answered, stroking his thick black beard. 'We're going to have to take a look.'

'In the dark?' Sly said.

'Do you want to wait until daylight when the marshal and the deputy are back here as well?' Jay asked angrily.

'No,' Sly said, shaking his head. 'That's no good of course, but we have to make our way past the soldiers to get into the mine.'

'I realize that,' Jay said coldly. 'I didn't say I was eager to do it – I said we had to unless we're willing to lose the money and let all of this count for nothing.'

'What do you have in mind, Jay? Storm in among them and cut loose?'

'We might be able to do that. There's only four of them. If we caught them by surprise it might work. They're half-drunk still and afoot, but I think we're better off trying to reduce the odds a little more. See if we can pick a few off one by one. What do you say?'

'That'll use up more time, Jay, and we still have the marshal and his deputy on our trail. But,' he admitted with a sigh, 'I guess we have no choice.'

'No,' Jay Champion said, coolly removing his Winchester from his saddle scabbard, 'I guess we don't. Let's get to higher ground and see how far they'll scatter. Never did know a horse soldier who could fight worth a damn afoot.'

'They're gone,' Private Boggs was saying. He, Cherry, Lassiter and Reese had scoured the campsite and nearby area in the gloom of night, finding nothing. 'For good, it seems. There's nothing left behind.'

Lassiter said, 'That was the point in driving off

our horses. They're long gone out on to the desert and we're standing here like fools. This is the last time any of us will ever talk the colonel into a three-day pass.'

It was the last time Lassiter would ever do anything. They saw him slap at his throat and simultaneously heard the near report of a rifle. The remaining soldiers dove for cover.

'Guess I was wrong,' Boggs said, panting as he lay next to Cherry behind a large boulder.

'Go up and get them!' Cherry said angrily. No one paid any attention to him. Charge unseen riflemen in the dark when the enemy had the high ground and, presumably, horses! Not likely. Cherry had shouted the order only out of frustration. He knew as well as anyone that it was an impossible task.

'We can't just stay here pinned down,' Boggs gasped. He lay on his back now, rifle held across his chest. 'They'll pick us off one by one.'

'What'd they come back for?' Reese asked.

'Us, it seems,' Cherry muttered.

'Why?'

'I don't know. Maybe they don't like the army. Maybe they're plain crazy.'

Boggs asked, 'What do you think, Cherry?'

'I think our best chance is just to split up and

make our way back to town. When the sun comes up we can formulate a new plan, maybe pick them off from cover if they show themselves.'

Boggs glanced toward the east. There was a narrow band of the faintest gray along the desert horizon. False dawn. If they did not make their break soon, they would find themselves pinned down in broad daylight. It would be a pure turkey shoot for the outlaws.

'If we're going to do that,' Boggs said, his breathing rapid and shallow, 'we'd better try it soon.'

'You're right,' Cherry agreed. His head was beginning to throb with the dull beginnings of a massive hangover. The last thing in the world he wanted to do was sprint for cover, but there was no choice. 'Did you hear that, Reese? They'll start shooting as soon as we rise up. Don't make it easy for them. Every man take a different route. We'll meet back at the saloon!'

Boggs was considering hopefully. There had only been one shot taken at them. Maybe the bandits had pulled out with sunrise not far away. He didn't believe it himself, but a man holds tightly to futile hopes in such a situation. Cherry raised his arm in a signal to be ready, and when his hand dropped the three remaining soldiers sprang to their feet and started at a dead run away from the mesa.

Four rapidly fired bullets followed them in their flight. Boggs glanced to his right and saw Reese fold up and crumple to the ground. He ran on as if the devil was on his coat-tails, fighting his way across the rough ground, through sagebrush, his only thought on the safety of the saloon. He didn't stop to see if anyone else had been hit. The soldiers were in full retreat.

The colonel would not be proud of them. Thank God he wasn't there to see his men, half-dressed, half-drunk, fleeing in the night like frightened children.

Boggs reached the flat ground first, stumbled and fell, slamming the breath out of his lungs. He scrambled to his feet, ducked into an alley and bolted toward the saloon, not pausing to look back for his comrades. Feet pounded behind him and he glanced that way to see Cherry on his heels, his bull-like body struggling for speed and breath. They hit the front door of the saloon nearly together and burst through to find three frightened females, their faces pale, eyes wide, waiting for them.

Cora Kellogg asked anxiously, 'Did you get them?'

Cherry said, 'Get me a glass of whiskey. Now!'

Boggs was crouched at the front window of the saloon, his rifle at the ready. Cherry accepted a glass of whisky from Cora with trembling hands and drank it down.

'We're the only ones left,' Cherry told her.

Laredo and Wage Carson heard the shots distinctly although they were a mile away from Hangtown when they were fired.

'Something's up,' Wage said, 'let's get going.'

The more experienced Laredo cautioned Wage, 'I'd rather get there with a live horse under me, Wage. Whatever has happened is already done, we can't stop it now.'

Wage admitted that Laredo was right. There was no sense in whipping the horses to reach an event that was already over. Still his impatience made it difficult for him to hold his gray to a walk. 'What do you think happened, Laredo?'

'Same as you,' Laredo answered. 'The soldiers tried to take it to Jay Champion.'

'Think it worked?'

'Why don't we wait and find out?' Laredo replied. Although if he were betting he would have put his money on Jay and Virgil Sly against three or four drunk horse soldiers. Whiskey was a

104

great equalizer.

The two reined up on the very same knoll that Laredo had rested on only the day before – was that all that it had been? The town was silent. No one was on the street, which figured. There were too many guns out there.

'What do you think?' Wage asked. Behind him now, as Laredo glanced his way, the first dully burnished colors of dawn were illuminating the eastern skies.

'Jay Champion. Virgil Sly. We've got to eliminate them. Or maybe I'm just speaking for myself, Wage. They're my responsibility, after all.'

'And mine,' Wage Carson said emphatically. 'They busted up my town.'

'All right then,' Laredo said, hiding a grin behind his hat as he wiped the sweatband. 'One thing we do know is that they'll be ready to make a break for it now. As soon as they recover the loot from wherever they've stashed it. There's still the other man – I think it must be Bert Washburn, from what I've learned of the gang. I don't have a good plan, but I have an idea.

'One of us circles up next to the shoulder of the mesa and Indians his way toward the camp. The other will have to be out watching if they've already pulled up stakes and broken for the desert. Which job do you want?'

'Flip a coin,' Wage said. It made no difference to him.

'All right. Heads, I win,' Laredo said without ever having produced a coin. 'I'll take the trail out. You try to get up behind them, Wage. If I hear shooting, I'll know for sure that they're still up there, and I'll be along to help you out. Same goes for you. If you hear weapons fired out here on the flats, you'll know they've made their run. In that case get back as quick as you can.' Laredo's face grew grim. 'I think I'd have a chance with any one of them, but with all three . . . just get back here fast if that's what happens.'

That was the way they decided to try it. With a startling flourish of color dawn blossomed, painting the eastern skies. With the same suddenness, the sky went white and empty again as day reclaimed the desert.

Wage Carson liked none of this. He was no warrior and knew it. He smiled, wishing that 'tails' had come up on the imaginary coin flip. He might have felt safer out on the open land than here, riding his horse through the deep cool shadows of the huge mesa, weaving through the scrub oak and manzanita. He was stalking three known gunmen and they had to know that he was coming.

Wage carried his rifle across the saddlebow. It was early and not yet sweltering, but sweat stung his eyes and pasted his blue shirt to his broad back. Hangtown lay stretched out below him. No one, nothing moved along its streets and alleys. It seemed as empty and devoid of life as it had the day he and Josh Banks rode into it.

But it was not empty, he knew. Somewhere down there were soldiers, women. And somewhere Liza sat watching or hoping, or afraid. She was safe now, or should be. But the situation was fraught with peril, and utterly unpredictable.

He would not allow her to be hurt. By anyone. Ever again.

Wage crested the low knoll he had been riding and reined in hard. His gray horse tossed its head angrily at the rough pull on the reins. Wage mentally apologized and stroked the horse's neck.

He was looking directly down at the outlaw camp. One man was visible, preparing his horse for riding. He had a pair of heavy saddle-bags in his hand. Now Jay Champion – for that was who it was – flipped them behind his saddle and fastened them there with hemp strings. The bank money, no doubt.

Wage shouldered his rifle and took careful aim, but Champion had gone to the far side of his horse, offering only a small target profile. But Wage had found him. The question was, where were the other men – Bert Washburn and Virgil Sly? Positioned in concealment ready to cut Wage down the instant he fired his Winchester? Caution caused Wage to examine the surrounding area slowly and cautiously. He saw nothing, heard nothing but – incongruously – the distant twanging of Gus Travers's banjo.

Where were Sly and Washburn?

As Wage tried to make up his mind whether to try to take Jay Champion out or not, the bearded bank robber swung into his saddle and started downslope toward town. Perhaps, Wage considered, he had missed his best opportunity, but not only did he not know where the other outlaws were, he had an inborn prejudice against gunning a man down without warning. Foolish he supposed; he knew it would be mocked in some circles.

Nevertheless, right or wrong he could not pull the trigger. He fell in behind Jay Champion, following him into Hangtown. Where were the other outlaws?

Jay Champion was also wondering where Bert Washburn was. If the kid had rabbited, at least he had left the money behind. But why had he failed to stay and guard it? After all, Bert was expecting his own share of the loot from the bank job. Jay could only conclude that the soldiers must have gotten Bert. It was a matter of little consequence to the desert hardcase.

Sly was a different story. Sure, at times he and Virgil disagreed, but the gunhand was invaluable, probably irreplaceable. No matter how tight the situation was, Jay knew he could count on Sly to stand and shoot it out. There was no rabbit in Virgil Sly's parentage, nor would a thinking man ever wish to find himself on the wrong side of Sly's gunsights.

Jay had heard no gunshots so he figured that things had not gone wrong. But had Sly had any success?

It was as they had neared the town limits the night before that Sly had suddenly pulled up and sat his quivering sorrel horse. 'My pony must have taken a bullet back there,' Sly said bitterly.

'When?'

'I don't know! How the hell would I know, Jay?

It's done, though. It might live, but it's not going to be able to make the run.'

'What do you want to do?' Jay asked.

'It's not a matter of what I want,' Sly said, swinging down from the sorrel, 'it's what has to be done. I've got to find another horse.'

'We pretty much eliminated all the extra horses in Hangtown,' Jay said dourly as Sly used an empty stirrup to swing up behind Jay Champion.

'Didn't we?' Sly agreed. 'That might have been the flaw in our plan. No matter – I'll find a mount if I have to ride a dray animal. It's past time we were out of here.'

'Hell of a fix,' Jay said, starting his horse toward the mesa, 'but then, Sly, we've been through worse and we're still here.'

So as Jay Champion had been busy recovering the hidden saddle-bags filled with thousands of bank dollars, Sly had slipped into Hangtown as dawn broke.

The saloon, Sly saw, was quiet. The hotel as well. There was a light still burning low in the marshal's office, but Sly knew that neither marshal nor deputy was there. He crossed the street, his shadow long and crooked before him and slipped into the alley next to the stable. There was a sudden discordant racket that caused

Sly to withdraw momentarily, hand on his pistol, before he recognized the sound for what it was.

Damned banjo.

Who played banjo at this time of the morning? At any time of the day or night, according to Sly's sensibilities, the instrument should be banned from the civilized world. Especially before breakfast. He crept toward the small back door of the stable, toed the door open and slipped inside, Colt revolver held barrel up beside his ear.

Once his eyes adjusted to the dim light, Sly was able to see a gaunt, silver-haired figure sitting on the tailgate of a Conestoga wagon, amusing himself with his vigorous plucking of his battered banjo.

'Party's still not over?' Sly asked, stepping forward.

'Who's that?' Gus Travers asked, peering into the murky shadows. He lowered the banjo and let it rest on his lap.

'You don't know me, friend,' Sly answered. 'Let's keep it that way.'

Sly glanced around and noticed the formless lump covered with a tarp lying in the corner shadows of the stable.

'What's that?' he asked.

'Man who tried to steal a mule.'

111

'Did you do it?'

'With what? The most dangerous implement I carry is this banjo,' Gus answered. 'It was the mayor who done it. It's his riding animal,'

Sly crouched and flipped the corner of the tarp back. It was Bert Washburn lying there. Sly grunted and stood. He glanced toward the open double doors and asked Gus, 'Where'd the mayor go?'

'How would I know? I'm party to no one's business but my own. Back to the marshal's office, I'd suppose.'

'All right,' Sly said displaying his Colt .44 again, 'here's what we're going to do. You are going to saddle that white-eared monster while I watch the street.' Gus slowly shook his head in a gesture of refusal, but Sly eared back the hammer of his pistol and the old man clambered down spider-like from the wagon's tailgate.

Sly knew that Jay Champion would be growing anxious, wanting to ride before the marshal and his lanky deputy showed up. He also knew that Jay would not run out on him. Not intentionally. Because no matter how far he ran, Jay knew that Sly would be riding in his tracks.

The two knew each other too well for treachery. The money mattered, but their outlaw pride mattered more.

Sly waited, staring into the white morning sunlight, glancing from the corner of his eye only occasionally to make sure the old man had no tricks to play. That seemed unlikely. Gus Travers had enjoyed a long life; he did not seem eager to terminate it. What did he care, anyway, about Josh Banks's mule?

Saddled, fitted with a bridle, the mule was led forward to Sly. The gunman frowned at the sight – for him to be riding a mule was a come down. He knew that many of the old-timers preferred them for their durability, but Virgil Sly on a beast that was half a donkey! No matter – he had to rejoin Jay Champion and blow off Hangtown. Things could only improve. With Dent and now Bert Washburn down, there was only the two of them to split what they had estimated to be twenty thousand dollars. There had been no time on the trail to sit down and count the cash, but twenty grand was a modest and fairly accurate estimate of their take.

The next few years would be taken in leisure in Mexico with pretty dark-eyed girls serving them drinks in the shade of *palmas*. The hell with Hangtown and its boy marshal. The hell with everyone. Sly yanked the reins to the mule from

Gus's shaky hand.

They were home free.

Or so he thought until he stepped outside and found the guns trained on him.

EIGHT

Wage Carson had reluctantly removed his gunsights from Jay Champion's bulky body. Still not knowing where the other two outlaws were he was reluctant to fire, and his focus had shifted to other concerns. That is, he knew where Jay was and had no real reason to take him down from ambush. If the outlaw leader did choose to make a run for it, well, Laredo was positioned somewhere along the road out of town. Champion was effectively hemmed in.

Wage was now more concerned about the town – his town. Had Bert and Virgil Sly slipped down there for some reason? To gather horses, for example. Wage was worried about Josh Banks now and, more deeply than he was willing to admit, about Liza.

115

He rode his gray horse down the sage-stippled slope and guided it toward the marshal's office. If anything was amiss, Josh would presumably know. Everything was still – silent in the dry heat of morning. Wage walked his horse toward the marshal's office. He saw no one in front of the hotel, no movement inside the saloon.

The quiet of the day held for only seconds longer.

Virgil Sly emerged from the stable, leading Josh Banks's white-eared mule. Across the street, Josh who must have been watching, came on to the porch of the marshal's office with his Winchester at his shoulder.

'Stop, thief!' Wage heard Josh shout, and then the loud crack of his Winchester rifle echoed along the street. Behind Wage two soldiers emerged from the saloon, rifles in their hands. Wage himself dived from the saddle to the powder-dry earth of the street as he recognized that the gunman, Virgil Sly, now crouched behind the mule, was ready and willing to fire back.

Sly's first two bullets drove Josh Banks to cover inside the jailhouse as his near shots pocked the adobe walls. Josh dropped his rifle and rolled inside, saving himself. The two soldiers were not so fortunate.

116

Private Boggs loosed a shot from his slow-loading .45-.70 Springfield in Sly's direction, missed and was shot as he tried to fumble another cartridge into the breech. From fifty yards away Virgil Sly caught Boggs in the heart with a bullet from his Colt.

Cherry had no better luck. The soldier's shot did nothing but stampede the mule, but Sly, firing from one knee, caught him with a bullet which went through the big trooper from side to side, and Cherry buckled at the knees and went down.

Sly grabbed for the mule's reins, felt the leather ribbons slip through his gloved hands and bolted for the shelter of the alley next to the stable. Wage Carson, afoot, went after him, letting the gray horse run free.

Sly, running on, cursed as long as his breath could sustain his anger. He thumbed fresh loads into the cylinder of his Colt as he ran, dropping a few of the brass cartridges in his haste. He slowed, closed the loading gate of his pistol and leaned against the heated wall of a building he took for the saloon.

Damn all! He had been so close. Now this.

But after all, he considered, there was no one on his trail but one hick marshal who knew what a gun was for but had never seen a master craftsman at his trade with a blue-steel Colt. The kid would blunder; he was bound to. Virgil Sly did not make mistakes when it came to shooting.

All right then, Sly thought, catching his breath. Take it to the marshal or wait him out? Sly decided to wait. The odds were better that way. Let the unskilled oaf stumble, slip, poke his head around a corner and he was done.

Better yet – Sly was thinking as he eyed the back door of the saloon – the kid was inexperienced enough to respect human life. Hostages might multiply Sly's chances enormously. He slipped inside the saloon and came face to face with Liza.

'Hello, kid,' Sly said with soft menace, locking the door behind him.

Liza tried to scream, but her constricted throat was knotted into silence. Sly put his callused hand over her mouth.

'Do you know who I am?' he asked.

'No,' Liza answered.

'The name is Virgil Sly. I've killed half a hundred men including two today. I am a man without mercy, kid. You do as I say and you might survive. Who's out there?' he asked, lifting his chin toward the saloon's ballroom. He relaxed his grip enough for her to answer.

'Just the girls.'

'No soldiers?'

'I think . . . I think they're all dead,' Liza answered. She held her head low, but her eyes were alight with dark fire. Sly lifted her chin with his thumb.

'You'd better be right. I don't like killing women – they have their uses – but it's been known to happen on occasion.'

He then forced her through the inner door toward the ballroom where the three other women, in various stages of dress and composure sat huddled near the whiskey barrel. Rebecca and Madeline registered astonishment; Cora Kellogg, whom nothing much surprised after her years hustling a dollar on the desert, only showed grim concern.

'Leave that young girl alone!' Cora shouted robustly.

Virgil Sly grinned an answer and shoved Liza aside. She stumbled, more with the unexpectedness of the movement than from Sly's force and fell to the plank floor.

'Y'all stand back just a few paces, ladies,' Sly said, gesturing with his pistol. 'I believe I could use a little sip of that honeydew myself just now.' So saying, Sly moved to the whiskey barrel and, using a glass which one of the girls had left there, he tapped it for a healthy double-shot.

'Awful stuff,' Sly commented after he had downed it. 'We used to sell better whiskey to the Indians.'

'What do you want?' Cora demanded brashly. Liza had managed to rise from the saloon floor and she dusted off her jeans, backing away from Sly as the others had done.

'Me, ma'am?' Sly replied, and it was difficult to tell if he was trying to be funny or not. 'I'm just wanting to leave this town in one piece. I thought you might be of some help there.'

The front door opened and Sly swung the sights of his pistol that way automatically. It was Cherry, who had somehow survived being shot through his body from arm to arm. He was bleeding profusely and angry. He did not seem, however, to recognize Sly as the man who had done the shooting. He lifted one hand toward Cora Kellogg and murmured, 'Cora, I need some help.' Then he folded up on himself and fell to the floor.

Cora looked at Sly for permission.

'Do what you can,' Virgil Sly said tightly. 'Hell, I had nothing against the man until he tried to gun me down.'

'Now what are you going to do?' the little firebrand of a girl demanded. Sly glanced at Liza, appreciating her nerve. The other women were lush and interesting, but they had shown no spine.

'I already told you, girl. I'm getting out of here. Someone is going along with me – maybe all of you. I don't want anyone, the marshal, that deputy, nobody else taking shots at me as I do so.'

'Virgil Sly, the notorious badman taking shelter behind a woman's skirts,' Liza shot back.

'Yes, miss,' Sly said after due consideration. 'There's a reason we come to be called notorious. Thank you for making up my mind. I'll take you. Let these . . . others sit here and cry in their lace handkerchiefs.'

'No you don't!' Cora Kellogg who had been trying to help Cherry shouted, 'Not the child. Take me, Sly.'

'You heard me, ma'am. I don't think this is time for a debate. I'm taking the youngster and going to the stable. Your man with the banjo is going to hitch up the surrey and I'm leaving town with the girl at my side.' His voice dropped to a low menace. 'Make sure no one follows after. It wouldn't be good for her safety.'

'You wouldn't!' Cora said, striding forward,

121

hands on her ample hips.

'Of course I would, ma'am,' Sly replied, refilling his whiskey glass. 'I'm quite – what did she say, notorious? – to my very core if my own well-being is in the balance.'

'You're cruel!' Cora shrieked.

Sly drank his whiskey and only smiled. 'Yes. Notorious and cruel. Do you think that a good woman could change me?'

If Sly's expression could be called a smile, it was the most evil smile Cora had ever seen. She had no doubt that Virgil Sly would do whatever it took to achieve his ends.

'All right,' Cora said trying to appease the homicidal Sly, 'I'll go along with you and tell Gus to harness the team.'

'That's all right, ma'am, I'm sure the little girl here can speak. I can't see why we'd need your assistance.'

Sly reached out a hand and grabbed Liza's arm, pulling her to him. 'Let's get going,' Sly said. To the others he said, 'You ladies stay here and stay quiet. Understand?'

Sly had entered by the saloon's back door. Now, however, with Liza as a hostage, he chose to leave from the front of the building. On the porch he paused for a minute to allow his eyes to adjust to the brilliant sunlight and to sweep the street with his eyes for Wage Carson. Where had the big deputy gotten to?

Satisfied that the way was clear, he shoved Liza on ahead of him and marched behind her toward the stable, gun held loosely beside his leg. 'Don't get any ideas,' Sly said with soft menace. 'I'd hate to have to nick you and have to carry you.'

'Where are you taking me?' Liza found the courage to ask.

'That depends on a number of things – mostly on how far anyone tries to pursue me.'

'The marshal will come after you,' Liza said forcefully. 'He'll never quit as long as I'm with you.'

'He'd better think that through twice.'

'What do you mean?'

'I mean,' Sly said, 'which way puts you in more danger? If he comes there will be shooting. If he leaves me alone I'll probably just drop you off a few miles down the trail.'

'You promise that?'

'No. I don't make promises, girl. Just remember to do as you're told and you should make out all right. I don't want to carry any extra baggage on the trail.'

They made their way to the relative coolness of

the stable under a white sky and eased into the shadows of the building, Sly letting his eyes search every square inch of the building before he was satisfied. Liza, just behind him, her arm still in his grip, trembled slightly. She did not like this man.

'What is it?' Gus Travers asked, peering out of the canvas flap at the rear of the Conestoga wagon. 'I thought I heard someone. Oh, it's you again! Didn't get far, did you?'

'I will this time. What'd you say your name was?' Sly demanded.

'Gus,' Travers said with an uneasy glance at Liza who was obviously being restrained.

'Come on out of there, Gus.' Sly ordered him. 'Don't get any ideas of gunplay.'

'Mister, as I told you before, I haven't a weapon of any kind, except my banjo. Though some people say my playing kills them.'

No one smiled in response to the weak joke.

'Just clamber on down,' Sly told him. 'I need you to hitch up that surrey out back. I assume those matched blacks are the team for it.'

'They are,' Gus answered. Rumpled, bleary-eyed after the long night and the morning's excitement, he clambered from the wagon, hitching up his suspenders over scrawny shoulders. 'Did Miss Cora give you anything by way of instructions for me?'

'She did,' Sly said in a low voice. 'She told me just to keep jabbing the muzzle of this Colt into your belly until you did what I asked.'

'Oh, it's like that, is it?' Gus said.

Liza interceded, 'Just do it, Gus, please!'

Gus hesitated, then said, 'All right, Liza.'

'Be quick about it,' Sly said, 'and quiet. Take the horses out back and we'll follow you.' They did follow Gus as he walked the matched black horses to the sun-bright alley where the surrey stood, but Sly, still holding Liza's arm in an iron grip, did not emerge from the shadows. He stood watching with his wolf eyes as the old man went about his work.

'Is there any water in here?' Sly asked Liza.

'I don't know. There must be, for the horses.'

'Find the water. Find a canteen and fill it,' Sly ordered as he suddenly released Liza, shoving her away from him. 'It's going to be a long hot day.'

Liza stood rubbing her bruised arm. 'All right. I'll try.'

Sly saw her eyes shifting to the double doors standing open at the front of the stable. 'Don't even think about running away,' he warned her.

'I wasn't thinking about anything except where to find a canteen,' Liza answered.

'Of course you weren't,' Sly said, stepping so near to Liza that she had to lean her head far back to look up into those savage eyes. His voice was nearly a whisper as he touched her shoulder as if with fondness and said, 'I once lived with a woman who looked something like you. We got along fine. Then one day she threw a little tantrum over something petty – I had told her to do something and she refused. She winged a half brick at my head.'

'What happened to her?' Liza asked weakly.

'What do you think?' Sly asked cruelly. 'Just do what I tell you, is all I'm saying, and we'll get along.'

Gus's nimble fingers were accustomed to the work he had been assigned and within another ten minutes the black horses had been hitched to Cora Kellogg's surrey. 'What now?' the old man asked, returning to the stable, dusting his hands together.

'Why don't you just crawl back up into the wagon and see how quiet you can be,' Sly said in a low growl. 'If you were lying to me about not having a gun, don't make the mistake of trying to use it.'

'I wasn't lying, and I wouldn't try to use a weapon on you if I had one,' Gus replied. 'But mister, can't you see your way clear to let the girl go now? You've got what you wanted.'

Sly didn't bother to answer. He gestured with his Colt, and Gus trudged across the stable to crawl up into the covered wagon again.

Liza had returned with a wooden canteen. 'I don't know how good the water is,' she told Sly. 'They were holding it in a rain barrel back there.'

'Any water's good water when you have none,' Sly said. He had ridden the desert too long to underrate its value. If it was a little brackish, too bad, but it was better than feeling your tissues slowly dry up, your tongue cleave to your palate, your throat grow constricted, your lips parch and split.

He did not think that he would have to travel far on that canteen. Jay Champion was also a veteran desert raider and he certainly would not leave the seep without full water-bags. Sly only had to get on to the trail to meet him. There was only the one way out of Hangtown. A few miles down the road the trail forked. The southern route led to Tucson, where they would most definitely not be heading since they still held the bank's money. The other angled westward, in the direction, he believed, of a patchwork settlement called Arroyo Verde. Although neither Sly nor Jay

127

had ever ridden that way, that would be the direction he would take. Jay would be along. Champion was his friend and would never cross Virgil Sly. And. . . .

Sly was the last man in the world he would wish to make an enemy of.

'Let's have at it, girl,' Sly said, slinging the canteen over his shoulder.

Clambering aboard in the sweltering heat Liza clasped her hands together between her knees, wishing for Wage Carson's rescue even as she prayed that he would not come. Sly would gun Wage down as soon as he saw the glint of the marshal's badge Wage Carson wore. Fearful though she was, Liza was nearly convinced that Sly would let her go once he had reached the safety of the long desert. After all, what further use did he have for her?

Sly slapped the reins against the glistening flanks of the matched black horses and the surrey lurched into motion.

The moment he heard the horses start, Gus leaped from the rear of the Conestoga and in a staggering run, made his way across the street toward the marshal's office. He was not a coward, he told himself. There was nothing at all he could have done to stop Virgil Sly. But he was not going to let the badman make off with Liza, sweet young woman that she was. Gus was very fond of the girl. There was no telling what a man like Sly might decide to do to her, given the time to consider the possibilities. There was little that was beneath Virgil Sly. Gus had seen his kind before.

Wage Carson had been explaining to Josh Banks, 'I chased him into the alley in back of the stable, but he just vanished. I decided to come back and check on you. I saw Sly firing at you, saw you take a tumble.'

'His lead didn't touch me,' Josh said. 'But it was damned close.'

'Where do you think. . . ?'

Wage looked around as Gus, panting with the exertion and the hot thin air of the day, burst into the marshal's office. Josh Banks rose from his desk, his weathered face drawn down with concern.

'What is it, Gus?' Josh asked.

'Liza,' Gus gasped, leaning against the wall, holding his tortured chest. 'Sly's got her.'

'Got her?' Wage Carson said with cold fury. 'Where? What do you mean?' For a moment Gus thought the brawny young marshal was going to hurl himself upon him. There was a fierceness in Wage's eyes he had never seen before.

'Sly made his way back to the stable. He's breaking for open desert in Cora's surrey, and he's got Liza with him as a hostage.'

'How did. . . ?' Josh began and then realized it was not the time for questions. Wage was already nearly to the door, snatching up his hat and rifle in passing. 'Wage!' Josh said in a nearly pleading tone. 'Be careful.'

Wage paused briefly at the open doorway to glare back at them. 'Save that advice for Virgil Sly. He had damned well better be careful, because if any harm comes to Liza I'll track him till I drop, if it takes following him to hell.'

NINE

Laredo frowned in concentration. The knoll on which he had positioned himself was littered with pocked, reddish volcanic rock and studded with scattered cholla – jumping cactus – their cat-whisker spines silver in the sunlight. Along the flanks of the knoll several tall, dry yucca plants stood, their white flowers faded and curled now, their seed pods brown and splitting.

Laredo was crouched in the only shade available – that cast by the body of his buckskin horse – peering down at the desert flats surrounding Hangtown. The four-passenger surrey was approaching him across the barren white sand.

Did that mean that the women had abandoned all hope of success in the ghost town? The black horses drawing the buggy were no larger than insects at this distance. There was a time when Laredo had carried field glasses in his saddle-bags. He no longer did, having decided that he was always going to have to draw nearer to his target to make a real assessment of the situation anyway. Just now he wished he had not given up the habit.

He restrained his curiosity and returned his gaze to the shadow at the base of the dark mesa. Jay Champion would have to make his run soon, and Champion was Laredo's objective. That and the bank money he would be carrying. Five years into this job Laredo had failed his employers only twice, and each time his failure had brought guilt and depression on its heels. Not that the bank examiner's office had ever reprimanded him; they knew that occasional failure was inevitable. Laredo, however, took failure quite personally and would relive each move he had made endlessly in his mind, wondering where he had made his mistake.

It wasn't that complicated, really. Once he had simply been outsmarted, the second time completely overmatched by the number of robbers he had been pursuing: the episode in Scottsdale when they had outflanked him and gunned him down in the street. Still, failure rankled.

He did not mean to fail again.

Where was Champion? For that matter, where was Wage Carson? He had heard shots earlier, but there had been no movement that he could see near the mesa. The weapons' reports had come from the town, then. Had someone managed to shoot down the young marshal? Wage had been told to keep an eye on the outlaw camp, but suppose he had been drawn off by someone? He might have drifted over to visit the little black-haired girl he was so obviously crazy about. Or perhaps one of the remaining soldiers harbored some sort of grudge against the marshal and had gone to shooting ... there was no point in speculating. There were too many possibilities.

Laredo determined that all that he could do was stick to the plan and keep watch for Jay Champion. The marshal would have to fend for himself.

He rose suddenly to his feet as the surrey swung westward. For now, emerging from the town limits of Hangtown, he saw a pursuer. The man, wide and thick, rode a gray horse, and he was riding hard. Why would Wage Carson be chasing the surrey? Something was up. Laredo settled his hat on his head and swung aboard the patient buckskin, starting it toward the western trail.

From the heavy shadow cast by the looming mesa, Jay Champion stood staring into the distances. His sorrel horse munched listlessly on the dry buffalo grass there. The black surrey had been driven out of town moments before, at breakneck speed before slowing on the long flats. That made no sense. If the women had been leaving Hangtown, they wouldn't have been in that much of a hurry. Besides, he had seen the figures of only two people riding the wagon. Unless something had happened to two of the women, something that had frightened them enough to leave town on the run . . . there was no point in speculating.

Minutes later Jay saw the thick figure of the marshal, rushing his gray horse toward the head of the town, pursuing the surrey. Who was he chasing? Again, there was no point in guessing about events. All that mattered was that the marshal was gone, in no position to trap Jay. The soldiers, if there were any left around, hadn't shown their heads. Jay Champion smiled with satisfaction. There was no one at all left to try to stop him.

It was time to make his break.

He gathered the reins to his sorrel and swung heavily aboard. He didn't worry about Sly. Virgil would know where he was heading. And, whatever the savage little man was up to, Sly would need no help in handling it. Jay Champion started down the hill, emerging from the deep shadows into the bright desert sunlight and struck out for the western trail toward Arroyo Verde.

Wage Carson's anger had cooled enough so that he could now force himself to slow the gray horse before running it to death. His anger had cooled, but not his determination. Nothing would happen to Liza – he would not allow it. Grimly he rode on across the rough ground and sandy washes. Sly had made his direction clear. He was taking the western road. A man on horseback might have eluded Wage, but the surrey needed to follow an established road. It was of no use over the broken ground beside the trail.

Recognizing this, Wage was able to gain on them. He did not need to wait until the road met the junction. Riding across country he could, with luck, reach the Arroyo Verde cut-off before Sly could.

The sun was white-hot on his back, the going rough over volcanic earth. The gray horse now and then tossed its head with annoyance, not liking the footing, but Wage urged the animal on. Dipping down into a wash, Wage found himself in a tangle of dry willow brush. He cursed as he fought his way through it. He had now lost sight of the surrey, but drove the horse on doggedly. He cursed himself for losing time in the long thicket, but he knew his instincts were correct. If he did not reach the road again in time to find himself ahead of Sly and Liza, then he would at least have gained much ground on them.

And that was enough. Sly might be quicker with a gun, a surer shot, but feeling as he did now, Wage would not hesitate to walk into the badman's sights and take lead if that was what it took to free Liza.

At last fighting free of the brushy tangle, Wage emerged on to the flats once again, in time to see the surrey, trailing dust, approaching him not a hundred yards off. He levered a cartridge into the receiver of his Winchester and sat his shuddering gray horse, waiting.

Laredo had watched the drama unfolding on the flats below him, and now he saw the big young marshal waiting for the approaching surrey. Still not sure who was riding in the carriage, Laredo frowned, spat drily and determined to go down to see if Wage Carson needed some help.

A moment later he had his mind changed for him.

The lone rider was slapping spurs to the big sorrel horse he rode. He too was heading toward the Arroyo Verde cut-off. It wasn't hard for Laredo to recognize the man even at this distance. He had been trailing Jay Champion for days.

Whatever work Wage Carson had cut out for himself, he would have to handle it alone. Capturing Champion and recovering the bank money took priority over all else. That was what they hired him to do, and he did not mean to trail back into Tucson ever again with the black mark of failure on him.

Laredo started his buckskin horse down the flank of the rocky knoll.

'Who's that?' Liza heard Virgil Sly mutter.. A string of oaths followed as the gunman yanked back the reins so hard that the suddenness of it caused one of the surprised blacks to rear high, pawing at the air.

137

Directly in their path Wage Carson had positioned his horse. He stood behind the gray, rifle across the saddle, muzzle trained on Virgil Sly.

'Drop your guns, Sly,' Wage ordered. Was it his imagination or was his voice a little shaky? He knew Sly's reputation, had seen some of his work first hand.

'What do you want?' Sly called back. Liza kept her eyes on Wage, hoping intently that he knew what he was doing.

'Just the girl,' Wage answered across the intervening distance which was no more than twenty yards. The gray horse stamped a foot and Wage prayed the big animal would stand, providing a bulwark against Sly's guns.

'Sure,' Sly replied after a moment's thought. 'Then what – if I let her go?'

'Then nothing,' Wage said meaning it. 'She's all I want. You can go on your way. You have my word for it.'

'He means it,' Liza said in a breathless voice. 'He's too honest to lie.'

'They don't make any men like that,' Sly said.

Still what choice did Sly have now? There was no way of firing past the horse. Skilled as he was, there was no clear target offering itself. What then? Trust the bulky marshal? Sly hadn't gotten as far as he had by taking anyone's word for anything. If he turned over the girl, what was to keep the marshal from opening up on Sly with that Winchester?

'I don't like it,' Sly shouted.

'I'm not asking you to like it,' Wage answered, 'I'm just telling you to do it. Let the girl go, Sly!'

'Put that rifle down. I'll walk her over to you,' the gunman offered.

'I don't think so!' Wage called back. Sweat trickled into his eyes. The sun was brilliant in a white sky. The heat of his horse's body was too near. Wage waited. Sly made no move, offered no response.

Suddenly Sly did move. 'All right, then!' he shouted. 'Her she is!' And Sly shouldered Liza roughly so that she tumbled from the seat of the surrey and fell headfirst to the ground. Simultaneously Sly drew his pistol and fired. His shot was aimed at nothing, was not meant to be. It panicked Wage's gray horse, however, which had been Virgil Sly's intent.

Wage who had watched Liza fall from the wagon was momentarily uncertain if Sly had shot her. At the same time his horse, taking fright, kicked out his heels and bounded on to the open desert beyond the trail.

Sly had started the matched black horses into a run, and he now bore down on Wage who had no choice but to throw himself aside, landing roughly on his shoulder. On the run, Sly winged two shots at Wage from the seat of the surrey. One of the bullets missed by inches, kicking powdered earth into Wage's eyes. The second one caught solid flesh, searing its way across Wage Carson's chest.

Sly drew the team up to finish the job.

Liza had risen and, screaming frantically, she ran toward Wage who lay twitching against the earth. Sly had clambered down from the wagon, and now with his hat tilted back he calmly reloaded his pistol as he strode toward Wage.

'Wage!' Liza shouted as she went to her knees beside the fallen marshal. He did not answer, could make no move to protect himself. Virgil Sly had just snapped the loading gate of his Colt shut when Liza scooped up Wage Carson's Winchester, steadied herself on one knee and shot the gunfighter through the heart.

Sly hadn't the time to say anything although his lips moved. He seemed, however, although it might have been Liza's imagination, to wink as he collapsed to the ground, already dead.

140

Liza bowed her head to Wage's body, searched for and found his steadily beating pulse, and rose quickly to catch up the black horses.

Returning, she managed to get Wage to his feet, but only briefly. He was murmuring words with no meaning through the pain. In a staggering walk they moved the ten feet to the surrey where she managed to topple the big man on to the back seat of the four-passenger rig. Panting with the exertion she went to the far side of the surrey, took Wage beneath both arms and tried to tug him all the way in. She couldn't do it!

The dry wind shifted her short dark hair. Liza stood up, breathing rapidly, shallowly. Walking to the other side of the wagon once again, keeping her eyes from the form of the dead Virgil Sly, she studied the situation. Wage's boots still touched the ground. He could not be roused from his pained slumber to assist her.

Again she tried to pull him farther into the surrey, her joints cracking as she strained against his weight. How does a man get so large! It was impossible for her to move him. The big oaf looked troubled in his sleep; blood stained his shirt. Giving in to an irrepressible urge she lowered his face to his and kissed him lightly. Wage lifted his arm and his eyes opened slightly.

She thought she detected a hint of a smile on his broad face.

'Wage,' she tried, 'Scoot up a little.'

Remarkably he did so, obeying Liza as if he were her child. Perhaps he was in a sense. The big blockhead.

Wage managed to pull himself into the surrey and then fell into unconsciousness once again. The dry wind whipped the tears from Liza's cheeks. She started the surrey toward Hangtown.

It took the three of them to get Wage upstairs into a hotel bed – Liza, Josh Banks and Gus. Josh and Liza did the best they could to bandage Wage's wounded chest. In Josh's opinion the wound which had bled copiously, was not life-threatening, but you never knew about gunshots, especially out here in the wilds where there was no decent medical aid and there was a constant threat of infection.

After Gus had gone Liza and Josh took up stations on opposite sides of the patient's bed and watched the big man pale with the loss of blood, inert and silent. The door to the room had been left open, but the window had been shut. A late afternoon windstorm had descended upon them and dust darkened the skies and coated the buildings of Hangtown with fine silt. The wind creaked and whistled, whispered and moaned through every opening like some evil omen.

'It's all my fault,' Liza said miserably. She held a handkerchief in her small hands, twisted as tightly as a rope.

'No,' Josh Banks answered. 'It's not, Liza. Don't start thinking that way. If anyone's to blame, it's me for letting him pin on that marshal's badge in the first place.'

'He would have come for me anyway,' Liza said, lifting dark liquid eyes to Josh Banks.

'Yes,' Josh said after a moment. 'I suppose he would have. No one's to blame then. Maybe it's just Hangtown – I can't see that this place has ever brought anybody any luck.'

The sandstorm had taken Laredo by surprise. He had seen Jay Champion veer off the road and strike out across country toward the Arroyo Verde cut-off, following very nearly the path that Wage Carson had used. Laredo, sensing triumph, urged his buckskin horse on to an even faster pace. Champion was not going to escape. Not this time.

He had seen the surrey boiling it toward town with a still figure thrown on to the rear seat. Wage Carson, it seemed, had met his match. That indicated to Laredo that Sly might still be waiting on the trail to join up with Champion. Or – had the marshal managed to take Sly down? That seemed unlikely, the big clumsy kid against a gunslick like Virgil Sly. But you never knew. When the bullets started flying, they had their own minds.

Still, Laredo rode with the assumption that both Sly and Champion were ahead of him, together or separately.

Now with the sky lowering, the first gusts of wind picked up the light sand and hurled it into Laredo's face. It would only get worse, he knew from past experience. No matter. He would not allow Champion to lose himself in the dust storm, he would not allow him to escape. The sky darkened, the wind increased, driving sand as stiff as buckshot against him. He could barely see the trail ahead of him now, would not have known if a hundred guns were positioned beside the road, waiting for him. He tugged his bandana up over nose and mouth and rode blindly into the swirling darkness of the hellish day.

TEN

The temperature rose, the gusting swirls of hot dust continued as Laredo rode on, trying not to lose the trail to the elements. He took only shallow breaths now, and his eyes were squeezed into a squint against the driving dust storm. He muttered curses, realizing that it was a futile waste of breath. Cursing men did no good and to threaten Mother Nature with a dry oath went beyond futility.

He had slowed his buckskin to a walk. He could not risk losing the path of the Arroyo Verde cut-off. That would leave him wandering aimlessly in the desert, miles from any hope of help. His only consolation was that Jay Champion could not be making better time under these conditions.

Nor Virgil Sly.

In this pelting, brownish haze, however, he could ride directly into their waiting guns if they had decided to pause and wait out the dust storm. Laredo's mouth was dry; his nostrils, despite the bandanna he wore, were clotted with dust. His eyes burned fiercely from the sandy assault of the wind.

His horse was faring no better. As the wind increased yet again, to a heated banshee force, he decided that he had no choice but to stop. The trail had grown invisible beneath drift sand. He halted reluctantly and turned his buckskin's head away from the wind. He, himself, squatted down between the horse's front legs and, hunched and weary, fearing that he might have lost yet another prey, waited out the blistering storm.

It was no time for dreaming, but as Laredo sat miserably against the desert floor, head bowed, he did spend a few minutes idly thinking about the course his life had taken, wondering if he should not have become a dirt farmer or a storekeeper – anything but the way he had chosen. His only consolation as the dreary minutes passed was that he knew that he had put some very bad men into prison and saved the money of other people – dirt farmers and storekeepers included – and kept them from ruin.

Dusk colored the sand-swept land vividly. Lurid purples and streaks of crimson clung to the storm as it passed. At the hour before sundown, the wind seemed to shift and lighten. Peering skyward, Laredo thought that he caught a glimpse of the coming half-moon through the dust veil.

He did not want to rise. He did not wish to ride into the teeth of the storm again, even if it was weakening, but there was no choice. Jay Champion and Sly would be riding at the first opportunity. On cramped legs, Laredo rose to his feet and with his eyes turned downward to avoid the brunt of the blasting sandstorm, he fumbled his way into the saddle again and turned the big buckskin horse westward once more.

The trail, though drifted with sand, was now obvious. The sky, still painted with rufous colors, was slowly clearing. The driven sand seemed more like an annoying swarm of darting insects than an assaulting force. And the half-moon could now be clearly seen, illuminating the cut-off.

Laredo rode determinedly on. He had no anger directed toward Sly and Champion. He simply could not fail. Maybe that said something about Laredo's own pride, his own needs. But he

147

would not fail himself.

He would not let Jake Royle down. If not for Jake, Laredo might have found himself at this very moment sitting in an over-heated cell in the Territorial Prison at Yuma. A man took care of his debts even if the obligation was to a dead man.

Laredo rode on.

The night skies were amazingly bright with stars sprinkled around the moon and scattered to the horizons. There was no breeze. Not a breath. The storm had vanished as quickly as it had arisen. From the rise, Laredo could see the pueblo of Arroyo Verde below, home fires bright in the windows of the few dozen adobe houses there. Beyond the town was the shallow canyon after which the settlement had been named. Green willow and tall, crooked sycamore trees grew along the watercourse.

Mentally, Laredo girded himself. He would see that his horse had water first. Then he would find the men he stalked. They had to be here, must be. How much farther could Jay Champion have ridden without rest? The bank robber would not go easy. Not simply hand over the money and surrender. It was going to be a shooting war, probably a killing time. So be it. Jay Champion had chosen his way of life as Laredo had chosen his. Now either or both must pay the price for those choices.

Entering the sleepy town of Arroyo Verde in the hour after sundown, Laredo scanned the dark streets. There was little activity. Those who lived here were not rough cattlemen, but family folks who would wish to be home for their evening meal. Light from the low adobe-block structures bled on to the red-rust street as Laredo walked his buckskin along its length, eyes searching the shadows.

Where would Jay Champion have gone first? Well, to a stable to see that his desert-weary horse was tended to. Laredo progressed until he saw a roughly carved sign above the door of a two-story structure. The sign was hardly needed to mark it as a stable. The straw and dung scent was heavy in the night. Laredo decided to swing down from his horse and walk it toward the building.

It made it easier to hold his Colt revolver.

Laredo had no doubts that any confrontation with Champion or Sly would lead to gunfire. Why would the bank robbers not fight? They had spent much time and energy sticking up the bank and escaping with their loot. They would not give it up without a battle. Not now.

The only slim advantage that Laredo had was

the fact that neither badman knew him on sight. Or so he believed.

Entering the darkness of the stable he paused, waiting for his eyes to adjust. There was no light to see by, only the distantly winking stars and hidden moon.

'Hello!' Laredo called out to the darkness, and Jay Champion popped up behind a stall partition with his pistol in hand.

Their two shots were triggered off within a split second of each other. Laredo spun, started toward the door as his horse reared up in panic. Then the stars blinked out one by one and the night went as black as night could ever be.

Morning light was a dazzle against the white wall of the hotel room when Wage Carson finally opened his eyes. He winced, closed them again and felt a comforting touch on his hand. Slender fingers, gently touching his grizzly-sized paw. He smiled first and then opened his eyes again.

'Liza.'

'It's me, you big lug,' she said. 'What were you doing, scaring us like that?'

'Was I scaring you? I didn't mean to. What was I doing?' Wage asked. He tried to sit up, failed and lay back again.

'All that bleeding and . . . oh, Wage! Are you going to be all right?' Liza asked, still clinging to his hand.

'Sure!' he said with a confidence he did not feel. Then he asked, 'What happened to me?'

'You faced down Virgil Sly. He won,' Liza said, thumbing tears from the corners of her wide dark eyes.

'He got away then?'

'No. We'll discuss all that later,' she answered. 'I think, Wage Carson, that you are the finest, bravest, most noble man I've ever known.' Then Liza dropped his hand, turned her back to him and marched out the door of the hotel room.

'I wonder why they do that,' Josh Banks said. It was only then that Wage noticed his old trail partner sitting in a shadowed corner of the room on a wooden chair.

'I don't know, Josh. But ain't it fine?'

When Wage next came around it was late evening. Josh had gone, but Liza was back with a bowl of bean soup. Like a motherly nurse, she propped him up on his pillows and spoon-fed him the bland but tasty concoction. They spoke not at all.

After fifteen minutes or so Wage could no longer keep his eyes open. He tried to apologize, did not know if he had succeeded or not, and then fell off again into a deep slumber.

When Wage awoke again, dawn had broken. Liza was there, but her face was drawn, her demeanor stiff and apparently calculated.

'What's the matter?' Wage asked from his bed.

'Nothing. What could be the matter? How are you feeling?'

'Fitter than I have a right to be,' Wage answered. Heavily he swung his bare feet to the floor. Liza backed away.

'Then I don't feel so bad,' she said hesitantly. Wage tried to study her eyes, but she turned them away from him.

'So bad?'

'Oh, Wage – I'm leaving. Cora's pulling out and I have to go with her.'

'Why?' Wage asked, rising clumsily to his feet. Liza backed farther away, her eyes brimming with tears.

'Because . . . because of what I owe her, Wage. And because—'

'Because?' Wage prompted.

'Where are *you* going, you big oaf!' she said, and then as if shamed, turned her back on him once again and rushed from the room.

Wage moved slowly to the window of the hotel

room and looked down, seeing Rebecca, Madeline and Cora Kellogg standing around the surrey. Gus was loading something on to the Conestoga wagon. Liza . . . was gone.

It was a struggle for Wage to tug his jeans on and to button his shirt, but he made it eventually, and went out into the warming glow of the early desert morning.

In time to see the little cavalcade disappearing around the corner of Hangtown to line out toward the desert flats.

Wage breathed their dust for awhile and then made his way heavily to the marshal's office.

'Well, then?' Josh Banks asked from behind the desk where he had been sitting with his boots propped up.

'She's gone,' Wage said wearily. He clogged his way toward one of the wooden chairs and lowered himself gingerly on to it.

'Did she say why?' Josh asked.

'She said she owes Cora too much. Said I'm going . . . nowhere.'

Josh didn't reply. There wasn't much to say to a man in love's misery. He did manage to mutter 'sorry' after awhile.

They sat in uneasy silence. The women were gone. Josh had buried Cherry that morning.

There was no one left in Hangtown.

'What are we going to do, Josh?' Wage asked dismally.

'I don't know, kid. I just don't know,' the old man admitted.

The sound of an approaching horse brought both of their heads up. Now who. . . ?

The door to the marshal's office swung open to admit a shaft of blue-white light.

And Laredo.

The tall man carried a pair of saddle-bags over his shoulder. He was trail-dusty and obviously weary, but he wore a smile as he marched to the desk and placed the saddle-bags on it.

'Got what I came for,' Laredo said.

'Is that the bank loot?' Josh asked, nodding at the saddle-bags.

'It is that,' Laredo said, seating himself in the other wooden chair. He glanced at the battered Wage Carson, but did not comment.

'How'd you get it?' Josh asked with interest.

'Off of Jay Champion's dead body,' Laredo told them. 'I trapped him – or he trapped me – in a stable in Arroyo Verde. He popped up and shot first. I thought I was dead, but I managed to fire back. Killed him.'

'Jay missed you?'

154

'Not exactly,' Laredo said. From his shirt pocket he removed a bright ornament. It was a deputy marshal's badge with a .44 caliber-sized dimple in it. 'Jay was a dead shot. I underestimated him. It was always Sly that I feared if it came to a showdown.

'Nevertheless, boys, here I am. And only because you allowed me to wear that badge. My heart, you know, was hiding just behind it.' Laredo paused, glanced at both men and then asked: 'What did happen to Virgil Sly, does either of you know?'

'Liza got him,' Wage mumbled.

'Well, then, there's nothing left to worry about,' Laredo said, stretching his arms. 'Men,' Laredo said expansively after having briefly turned away, 'I feel that I owe you something for your help. I was thinking about this along the trail, now I would like to make you an offer. How would you like to work for the Territorial Bank examiner's office?'

'And do the job you do!' Wage said. 'I hardly think so, Laredo. Thanks all the same. Getting shot up once is enough for me.'

'You misunderstand me,' Laredo said. 'There are now fourteen banks in the city of Tucson. There are jobs going begging as a bank guard. It is simple work, and the risk is not really that great. One bank out of fourteen suffers an attempted robbery every six months or so. The rest of a guard's time is spent opening doors for old ladies or filling ink wells.'

'I'm a little too old even for that,' Josh said. 'My legs are no good, my eyes even worse.'

'I considered that, too, Josh,' the tall man told him. 'A bank, like any other business needs maintenance. A trustworthy man who can push a broom for a few hours a night is considered an asset – unless you think the job is beneath you.'

'Son,' Josh Banks said, 'no job that pays is beneath me.'

'We'll discuss it on the road to Tucson,' Laredo told them. 'If you change your minds, that's your business. I just wanted to make the offer.'

Wage wasn't sure one way or the other. His future made no difference to him. He only wished that Laredo had returned with that offer before Liza had rolled out of town with the others. Maybe that would have been enough to change her mind – some sort of stability in her vagabond life.

The sun was riding high when the three men started for Tucson. Behind them Hangtown

156

seemed to groan and resume its slow collapse.

'Well, that was a grand experiment,' Josh commented. 'I guess we weren't meant to own our own town.'

'I guess not,' Wage Carson answered. 'I don't know if I'll like Tucson, but they must at least have some sort of food there that's an improvement on venison and beans.'

'I suppose so,' Josh said, halting his mule for one last glance back at Hangtown. 'It's a shame and a pity, but I suppose nothing good can ever come out of Hangtown.'

But as Wage also looked back and surveyed the ghost town, he saw that Josh Banks was wrong.

The little girl with the huge dark eyes was standing at the head of the street, waving frantically after them. ✦